A Collection of Short Stories

PORTRAITS OF THE PEN

First published by City Limits Publishing 2020

Copyright © 2020 by City Limits Publishing

All rights reserved. No part of this publication may be reproduced, stored or transmitted in any form or by any means, electronic, mechanical, photocopying, recording, scanning, or otherwise without written permission from the publisher. It is illegal to copy this book, post it to a website, or distribute it by any other means without permission.

This novel is entirely a work of fiction. The names, characters and incidents portrayed in it are the work of the author's imagination. Any resemblance to actual persons, living or dead, events or localities is entirely coincidental.

City Limits Publishing has no responsibility for the persistence or accuracy of URLs for external or third-party Internet Websites referred to in this publication and does not guarantee that any content on such Websites is, or will remain, accurate or appropriate.

First edition

ISBN: 978-1-954403-41-3

Editing by Robert Martin
Editing by Lily Peterson
Cover art by Jelleine Joie

Contents

Dedication	iv
Editor's Note	v
Paxton's Socks	1
The 70-Year Itch	8
Foundling	16
The First Meeting	23
Who Needs A Helping Hand?	27
A New Kind of Virus	35
School Day	41
The Window	48
The Last Supper	52
The Swoozlemunger	55
Lucky Seven	60
Blind Optimism	63
An Uncommonly Sunny Day	70
Save the Date	76
Love and Loss	83
Black Death	89
The Old Man	96
The Beach House	100
The Orchid	105
Disappearing Act	109
About the Authors	116

Dedication

To the stories yet to be told and the characters yet to be written. May the portraits of the pen contained within these pages inspire new tales.

Editor's Note

City Limits Publishing has had the distinct honor to work with the two dozen authors represented in this collection of short stories. Their stories and voices are powerful and their words paint such vivid pictures. We would like to thank them all for their participation in this collection.

Works of Note:

Overall Winners:
    1st Place - *Paxton's Socks* by P.A. Richardson
    3rd Place - *Lucky Seven* by Claire A Murray

Category: Fiction
    2nd Place - *The Orchid* by Eric Ryan

Category: Suspense/Thriller
    1st Place - *The First Meeting* by Raissa Batra
    2nd Place - *Foundling* by Barbara Herrera

Category: LGBTQ
    1st Place - *The Last Supper* by L. Player

Category: Life Lessons
    1st Place - *School Day* by Milo Cumaranatunge

2nd Place - *Save the Date* by Barbara Herrera
3rd Place - *The Window* by Adam Silver

Category: Romance
1st Place - *The Beach House* by Mary Jane Hill
2nd Place - *An Uncommonly Sunny Day* by Ramona Scarborough

Category: Young Adult
1st Place - *A New Kind of Virus* by Carrington Parrott

Paxton's Socks

Written by P.A. Richardson

The picture made the front page of the newspaper.
    The consensus among my neighbors was that the evil radiated from him so strongly that one could see the malignant glint in his eyes. A consensus doesn't mean everyone thinks the same thing, though; it just means enough people share the same opinion that any reasonable person—a judge, perhaps—would conclude that there was a general agreement.

I'm eighty-four and I've never been accused of being reasonable. I'm stubborn and difficult and I love a good argument. I've been known to derail a perfectly pleasant Sunday dinner by serving a healthy portion of politics before dessert. If Betty Milbourn has an opinion, I will express the opposite view, just to get her agitated. Not this time. I let my friends have their opinion and I didn't bother them with the truth. And the truth is, the only thing that picture showed was a young man in a county jail jumpsuit, standing next to a stranger who was paid by the state to defend him.

#

My bungalow in a retirement community is utilitarian, nothing fancy. The biggest benefit for me is that it is a cooperative, meaning someone else does the yard work and heavy maintenance. There is a community center, where I can play cards or board games or watch a television program that doesn't interest me at a volume that assaults my ears.

It's not assisted living—I get around okay. I can navigate my little house and take care of myself, but I need help with some housework. I can still do complicated math in my head, but I don't trust my balance on a step stool. I use one of those do-good agencies to help me with the things I can't – or don't want to – do anymore.

It seems like every few months I annoy or intimidate a helper too much and the agency sends someone new and I have to start over. That's how I met Paxton. He showed up one day, informed me the agency had sent him and asked, rather formally, if I would like him to read to me. "Or we could watch TV. Or talk, I guess."

He looked so earnest, with his sport coat and penny loafers, that I burst out laughing. "What's your name, son?"

"Um, Paxton?" His confusion turned it into a question.

"They didn't tell you anything about me, did they?"

He shook his head.

Figured. The endless stream of Brittanys and Haileys they sent to me proved they were just plugging time slots with bodies without regard for the client's requirements. "They just said you like to read, so I thought… I mean, that's what I do with the other clients. But they didn't say anything else."

"I can read just fine, Paxton. I need help with some housework, things I can't do easily anymore. Today, Brittany – or Hailey, whatever her name was – was going to clean the kitchen floor. I have a bad back. We can talk while you work if you feel like it." He sized me up, a little smirk at the corner of his mouth.

I stared back.

"You're serious? Okay, boss," he said. And he kicked off his loafers, rolled up his sleeves and scrubbed the floor with a wood-back scrub brush, on his hands and knees. He didn't complain about it, either, or do a sloppy job. Definitely an improvement over the last Hailey.

He showed up, without fail, every Monday and Thursday for the next eight months. On time, every time. Paxton always looked put-together, spiffy, as I call it. I only saw him in jeans once, and he still managed to look like he was on his way to a business meeting. His square glasses gave him a preppy, serious appearance, but he also had a collection of novelty socks. My favorites were the sloth socks.

"You gotta have the look. If you want to get somewhere, you gotta look like you belong," he told me. I didn't disagree, which is why the novelty socks delighted me. It was a subtle nod at the ultimate absurdity of life's social rules, for which I have little respect.

Paxton shared the grand plan with me. Graduate college next semester, become an EMT, marry the girlfriend, and then apply to the police department.

"Why become an EMT first?" I asked.

"It fascinates me. Like, if I saw a car crash, traumatic injury —"

"So, you could help?"

Paxton laughed, a cynical chuckle. "Exactly. People are stupid. They'll always need help."

"I guess I don't understand the connection between EMT and cop. It seems like an odd path to take if the end goal is the police department."

Paxton nodded. "Maybe, but it's still good experience, and

that kind of stuff interests me. Have you ever seen those fail videos online?"

"What is a fail video?" I asked. "I don't think I want to know."

"They're hilarious. There's tons of them that show people doing crazy stupid stuff. Like this one guy jumps off his roof onto a trampoline, trying to land in the swimming pool, but he hits it wrong and he lands like twenty feet away in the bushes."

"That doesn't sound hilarious. That sounds painful. And dangerous."

Paxton shrugged. "Guy shouldn't have jumped off the roof. Stupid."

I frowned at his tone. We often debated current events and politics, so I assumed he was being contrary to bait me into one of our mock arguments. But I couldn't be certain.

When he heard me whistling a pop tune one afternoon, he looked surprised and said, "You know that song?"

"How am I whistling it if I don't know it?" I snapped. That would have sent one of the Brittanys back to the agency with a complaint about how nasty I am, but Paxton just laughed.

"You know what that means? Cake by the Ocean?"

"I just like the tune. But since you seem so shocked, it's probably about sex. Your generation didn't invent that, you know. You didn't invent singing about it, either."

"Damn, boss," he said with a slow drawl.

After that, Paxton showed me how to make a playlist of some of my favorite songs and how to play it from my phone, or my portable radio—the magic of Bluetooth—and even in my car that I am not supposed to drive anymore.

A few weeks later, Paxton showed me a new spider web tattoo on his elbow. A tiny yellow spider was in the top left corner. It looked unprofessional, like an eight-year-old had drawn it.

"Why a spider web? Are you the spider? Or the bug?"

"I got it for my birthday. I just liked it, doesn't mean anything," he said.

Some lies land gently in a conversation like a butterfly alighting on a flower petal. Some lies crash a conversation like a tower of dinner plates. That lie felt like the entire china cabinet had tipped over and smashed on my floor, but Paxton changed the subject before I could ask another question. It clearly meant something to him, but I didn't want to push.

My husband has been gone for fifteen years. My son calls sometimes, but he hasn't visited in over ten years and I haven't seen my grandchildren since they were teenagers. Life is mobile now and I am less willing to try to keep pace. My grandkids are polite and kind, but they have nothing to say to an old lady. I love my son and I can tolerate his wife, but our lives are separate and the connections, always tenuous, finally drifted away. Paxton filled that space for me and so I let him keep his secret about the tattoo. It didn't matter to me.

That evening, I got online and ordered two pairs of novelty socks for Paxton's birthday – cats wearing bow ties and pink flamingos. With express delivery, they would arrive within a week. I couldn't wait to give them to him. I thought he would like them, considering his love of the goofy sloth socks.

The next time I saw Paxton, he was in a foul mood. He brushed me off when I asked what was wrong. "This whole fucking week has been horrible." Although I drop f-bombs like I'm a bombardier — one of the perks of being over eighty — Paxton never swore around me.

"Girl trouble?" I asked.

"Always," he replied, and laughed.

It was the laugh that threw me off. I allowed it to fool me. I thought he was just having a bad day. There probably aren't a lot of nights left in my future, but I doubt another one will pass that I don't regret not pursuing that conversation.

#

Paxton didn't show up the next Monday. I called the agency, but the girl who answered the phone hemmed and hawed and left me on hold so long that I finally hung up. With nothing to do and no one to talk to, I walked the half block to the community center.

"So sad. That poor family."

"What if it had been one of us?"

"You just never think that could happen."

The murmured conversations stopped when I walked through the door. I ignored them and went straight for the coffee table and the newspaper. They were probably talking about Millie Davis again. Last week, she walked outside stark naked and had no idea what the fuss was about. She rode off in an ambulance and my guess was that she would end up in a memory care center. I'm not interested in gossiping about someone's misfortune. At this point in my life, I don't need that kind of karma.

I set aside the entertainment pages.

"What if it had been poor Barbara? She took a liking to him, I think."

Dimly, my brain reacted to hearing my name, but I was staring at the front page. Paxton in a jumpsuit. Those square glasses caught the glint of the lights. I couldn't see his eyes because of the glare, but he looked defeated. His shoulders were hunched forward. VALLEY VIEW MAN ARRESTED IN SLAYING OF EX-GIRLFRIEND. I read the story twice, but I still couldn't make sense of it. I couldn't reconcile the facts in the article with the young man I knew. There was no question that he stabbed his ex-girlfriend – he never told me they broke up – because the police found him with the knife, sitting next to her body. I left the community center without saying goodbye to anyone.

When I got home, I checked the mailbox out of habit. Three bills and a small package. Paxton's birthday socks. He had just turned twenty-two.

The 70-Year Itch

Written by Andy Wasif

The ticking of the miniature grandfather clock centered on the mantle seemed to grow louder, each pass from the pendulum a hatchet to the silence of the living room, which itself spoke loudly as a docent, guiding us through a family's history. The clock was a wedding present from Aunt Mabel, purchased in 1940 during a train trip to Chicago and kept on her own mantle before passing it along. The azure-colored chair with the black trim, a 1960s-era beauty, still in good shape, virtually untouched, seemed out of place set aside from the more modern Macy's sofa with black cushions you could get lost in that framed the white-lacquered coffee table peppered with aging *Readers Digest* magazines.

Hanging on the walls and displayed next to the clock, this exhibition's depth was captured by discount store frames highlighting the family through the decades: that trip to Paris where he proposed; the formal bride and groom pose at the Spring Valley Country Club; a portrait of her holding a rosy-faced newborn; their eldest in his Little League baseball uniform; a portrait of the entire nuclear family, now totaling four, from Sears with a backdrop of green, brown, and yellow, defined by polyester pants and pointed collars; and finally, one similar, this in high definition, showing an aged couple with their expanded family - three generations

of Mitchells, the couple from the start flashing a smile in direct opposition to the pair that now sits across the room at the dining room table.

The present versions of themselves, Hy and Sylvia, now in their 70s, stare at each other with passion. That is, a passionate distaste. Hy's forehead creases angrily, driving his eyes downward, his breath escaping through his deviated septum steadily with a slight wheeze between every third tock of the clock as he sits hunched over his dinner plate.

Equally, Sylvia's mouth clenched, her back molars locked in a struggle for supremacy. Her head angled away, she glares through the corners of her wrinkled eyes, suspicious and skeptical of his very existence.

Finally, after an inordinate amount of time when even the cooling meal in front of them felt uncomfortable, Hy speaks. "Hag," he says with purpose, as if he'd prepared just the right word for the occasion.

"Bastard," Sylvia counters, as a tennis pro would effortlessly volley from inside the service boxes.

And again, they fall prey to the clock's syncopated rhythm, the tea vapor visibly dissipating into the atmosphere.

And then. . .

"I know what you're doing to me," Hy says in a *"J'accuse!"* moment.

Unswayed, Sylvia replies, "What am I doing to you? I made you a nice meal with potatoes, brisket, green beans…" Each food a pointed indictment of his tone.

Hy interrupts, "Nuts!"

She rolls her eyes at his paranoia - those gray-blue eyes with specks of brown that he used to write poetry about, albeit bad poetry. "There are no nuts!"

Gaining confidence, Hy says, "There are nuts! Pine nuts, walnuts…"

Sylvia nods. *Ah, so this is how we're gonna play it*, she thinks. "So what if there are?"

"You know it wreaks havoc with my colitis."

"You don't… have… colitis," she says for the umpteenth time. If she didn't know any better, she'd swear smoke was coming from her molars.

"I don't need a doctor to tell me what I have," Hy claims for the umpteenth plus-one time, clenching his fist. He's sure her constant argumentative state is the cause of his arthritis.

"My father had it, my brother had it, I have it." Sylvia doesn't dare continue. What's the point? She reaffixes her gaze at him, as if they'd invented a surgery that replaced her retina with disintegration lasers. And Hy focuses all his energy on her, boring a hole in her with his mind.

Sylvia breaks the silence this time. "Sonuvabitch."

"Shrew."

Sylvia leans in, launching her offensive. "Don't think I don't know what you're doing either."

Hy's eyes grow wide and innocent. *Oh, really? My hands are nowhere near the cookie jar*, he thinks. Her claims are but baseless speculation. "I'm doing nothing."

"Flirting with your tai chi instructor is nothing?" Sylvia's eyes narrow.

"What flirting? She helps me to touch my toes."

"Does she have to stand so close?"

"It's the nature of the beast."

Sylvia throws her hands up in the air. "50 years, I've never known what that means."

"It means just what it says," Hy says, a favorite response of his and distant relation to his trite parenting phrase "Because I said so."

"Well, that doesn't help."

Hy's stomach begins to churn like large vats of cream at a Dreyer's factory. "You're giving me indigestion."

A little giddy at the thought, Sylvia snaps, "You deserve indigestion."

Hy sits up sharply and says, "And you deserve-" His mind races to come upon any witty and pointed rejoinder for several beats before losing interest with a disinterested wave of his hand. "Meh!"

They reposition themselves in silence, shorter in duration this time as Sylvia senses her husband wearing down. "Gasbag!"

"Hygienically-challenged fussbucket!" Hy says, surprising even himself with such a gem. He sits back proudly and crosses his arms.

The woman he had for many years sweetly called "Syl" flicks a snap over her head. "You've got nothing to complain about in the wife department," she says.

This plays right into Hy's hands. He reaches past his faded argyle vest and into the breast pocket of his one-size-too-large department store shirt. "I'll show you 'nothing to complain about'... I've got a list." And with that, he pulls out a piece of paper, folded into credit card size, fraying around the edges. Clearly, it's been his companion for a while.

The reveal doesn't seem to surprise Sylvia who waits in anticipation of Hy's grand production as he retrieves his bifocals from his vest pocket and tries to flick them open with the flick of a wrist. They don't budge. After four attempts, he grabs one earpiece and opens them manually. Sylvia lets out a heavy, impatient sigh. "Yeah, put your cheaters on." Hy ignores her comment, instead focusing on the matter at hand.

"Number One," he says, pausing for suspense, "-the first fifteen years... Number Two – Paris."

Sylvia shakes her head, almost feeling sorry for him. "Still with the Paris!"

"I should have left you at the Eiffel Tower."

"I should have jumped." Sylvia one-ups him again.

Hy puts his list aside and leans against the table, his sleeve catching a bit of mashed potatoes. "You think you got it so bad?

"You bet your trick knee, I do. I got a list!" And with that she reaches down her housecoat to pull out a note card from deep in her bosom.

Hy throws his head back and lets out a guffaw, the sudden movement causing a sharp crick, a sensation radiates through his neck. He grabs it, hoping Sylvia doesn't see. "This should be rich," he says.

She takes the bifocals from around her neck and puts them on. From the front of the card, she reads, "Number One – You never listen to me!"

Hy's taken aback by this. "Never listen to you?! I hear you in my sleep!!"

Undeterred, Sylvia flips the card over, "Number Two – Paris."

"You stole 'Paris' from me!"

Sylvia says, "I should have never gotten in your car."

"I should have kept on driving." He feels his sweater start to irritate his skin as his temperature rises. He and his wife of fifty years settle back into their default positions, nostrils flaring, until the intermission ends quickly, Sylvia now just toying with the timing to catch Hy off-guard.

"Loser."

"Witch."

"Faggot!"

Hy gasps. "That was one time!" he says, hurt that she would dredge up the drunken collegiate costume party when he asked out a fair-skinned football player in a cheerleader's outfit, a mistake he has regretted twice -the night of the party, and the time he told her about it.

Having him on the ropes, Sylvia indicts him. "You promised me a house…"

He looks around at their comfortable surroundings. "What, are we living in a box?"

Sylvia continues, "…on a hill, a house on a hill."

Hy squares up his body to the table. "Oh, I see. You want a hill? I'll give you a hill." He picks up his fork and slices the tines through the pile of mashed potatoes, now cold among the green beans and brisket in front of him. He scoops some of the potatoes onto the fork. He always loved that Sylvia makes it with lumps, but never more than he does at this moment as the starchy side dish doesn't run through the fork. He turns the fork back to him like it's a miniature Jai Alai basket and, without any pretense, spikes the food right into her water glass.

Sylvia cowers for a moment, but her fear quickly returns to anger, with double the intensity, twice the fury. "How dare you?!" She picks up the glass of mashed potato water, her fingers gripping it so tightly her age spots seem to whiten, and she flicks the glass so the water sails out toward him, though wide left of his head. He whips his head around to see it land harmlessly on the carpet behind him, sinking into the microfibers.

Now seething as well, he turns back to her. "I'm glad you did that!" Hy pushes his chair back, its legs sputtering along the Persian rug beneath the dining room set. He stands, steadies himself, and then lifts a leg toward 30 degrees, as if to take a step, before placing it back down in front of him. Then he makes a controlled swipe forward with his left arm, and bringing that back, he swipes forward identically with his right arm, as if swimming in molasses in a Tai Chi movement called, "Working the Pulley." Then he brings both arms over head before releasing them to his sides. Hy finally begins to feel comfortable after six weeks of practice. "I've wanted to do this for fifty years."

"If you want a fight, you've got it, buster." Sylvia tries to extricate herself from the table, but has trouble, her knee banging into the table leg as her chair catches on the rug she now regrets purchasing. She continues to struggle as Hy repeats his taolu across the table.

"Prepare to get the beating of your life."

"I'm gonna tear you apart," she says, still struggling. After a moment of trying to figure out why her chair won't move, she looks up at him. "Help me up." Hy puts his tai chi behind him and shuffles over to her. He lifts the corner of the table, just enough for the rug to give way and for Sylvia's leg to gain its freedom. He leans over her. She puts her arms around his neck and he grabs around her back.

"On three, we're gonna stand. One, two. . ." and on "three," he shifts his weight back as Sylvia springs up, her foot catching on the table leg, which sends her stumbling into his arms. When she regains her balance, she looks up to see Hy's eyes a nose away from hers. They stare at each other, their hot breath crashing against each other's mouths like waves at the base of a stately lighthouse, stirring the memories of a thousand caring moments forged over five decades of love.

Sylvia smiles. "You know what this reminds me of?" A warm tone of pumpkin spice awash in autumn colors that has always had the ability to melt Hy's heart.

Hy nods and tilts his head to kiss her ever so gently on her lips. "Paris."

Foundling

Written by Barbara Herrera

Chalcey had always been mild. Everything was comfortable: the temperament of its citizens, the heat of the summer days, and the chill of the winter nights. If moderation was something to be proud of, Chalcey would be known far and wide. As it were, there was nothing worth noting. Not until the silvery slump was found in the middle of the town fountain.

It was the twins who found it first. Jacob wanted to sneak up on it, but Cody couldn't help but blurt out: "What the hell is *that*?!" The creature almost looked like a small child, playing in the water, but as the boys grew closer, they noticed the differences. This child was a silvery-white color, without a single hair on its body. Its bones protruded through its skin, as if it had never had a good meal in its life. Perhaps most concerning, the child didn't seem to have any genitals.

Jacob poked the child with a stick he found on the ground. When it slowly turned its face to him, he asked, "What are you?" He didn't mean to be crude; at ten years old, he wasn't the most tactful. In place of an answer, the child only blinked. Its eyes looked as empty as the night sky, devoid of emotion or feeling or soul.

Jacob asked again. "I *said*, what *are* you?"

Silence.

"Well, can you get up at least? Let's have a look at you."

The child slowly raised to its feet and turned to face the boys. It looked like a doll, one that hadn't even been given the dignity of clothes or hair. It wasn't a cold day, but the boys had the warmth of their dry clothes. They felt bad for the child. It had nothing.

Cody turned to his brother. "Should we give her some of our clothes? I mean, it's not proper to be naked in the middle of town."

Jacob made a face at his brother. "What makes you think it's a girl?"

"Even if it's not a girl. It's *naked*, Jacob."

Jacob sighed and took off his shirt. He was about a foot taller than the figure, so the shirt that barely came down to his belt was practically a dress for this thing. It would have to do. They helped it dress and Cody took over the role of talking to the child.

"We're going to take you to the mayor, friend. He'll know what to do with you." He smiled in an effort to make the child more at ease. The child only blinked. There were only a hundred yards or so between the fountain and the town hall, but the child's small, frail legs didn't move very fast. Every dozen or so paces, the boys would stop and wait for it to catch back up. It was unclear whether the child understood the words they said; no matter what they said to it, it never opened its mouth in response. Still, they kept talking amongst themselves.

As they walked, people started to gather outside. The whispers started quietly, but soon grew. *What is that thing?*

What have the Herkel boys done now? Whose child is that? No one had any answers, but still the townsfolk traded questions.

By the time they reached the front steps of the town hall, the mayor was out front waiting for them. Jacob spoke first. "We found *this thing* in the fountain." He motioned to the child, while Cody continued for him.

"We want you to help us find her parents."

Immediately after, Jacob chimed back in. "It doesn't talk, either."

The mayor looked the child up and down carefully, not immediately sure how to continue. "Wow. You're an ugly little thing, aren't you?" The child blinked. The mayor turned back to the boys. "I'll tell you what. Why don't you leave her here with me? I'll get her some more fitting clothes, and I'll see what I can do with her."

Cody was hesitant, but Jacob pulled him along anyway. "I mean, I'm sorry for it and all, but c'mon, Cody. It's not our problem anymore." Cody supposed he was right.

As the boys walked home, the mayor pulled the child into the hall. He called up his assistant to help come up with something to do with the child. It just wouldn't be proper for a *male elected official* to be alone with an *underdressed female runaway*, either. The people might suspect something uncouth.

When the assistant entered the room, she tried to stifle a gasp, but was unsuccessful. The child only blinked. Reluctantly, she held out a hand, and after staring at it for an uncomfortable length of time, the child reached out to grab it. As she led the way out of the room, the child walked slowly behind her.

With the child being attended to by his assistant, the mayor began to make some calls. His first thought was that this thing was clearly inhuman; perhaps they could market it as an attraction and boost the local economy. Even if she was human, there was clearly something off about her. He called up the doctor to explain the child's situation. They agreed it would be easier to examine her in person, and the doctor hung up.

Instead of coming alone, the doctor brought along a scientist colleague. "If this creature was as unique as you say," he explained, "then it's worth a thorough look." The mayor was displeased, but allowed the scientist to enter, too. Soon after the men gathered, they were joined by the assistant and the child. The woman almost looked as if she feared the child; truthfully, she hadn't decided what to think yet. The child only blinked.

The doctor spoke to her first. "I'd like to take a look at you, if that's all right." The small child stared hard at his face, almost as if she was looking straight through him to the wall behind. When she said nothing, he held the stethoscope up to her chest. The rhythm was off just slightly; instead of thump-thump, thump-thump her heart went thump… th-thump, thump… th-thump. She wasn't warm to the touch, either, even under the thick sweater the assistant had found for her.

The doctor checked her eyes, which were as vacuous and unresponsive as he expected them to be. She refused to follow his flashlight, and it didn't seem to bother her at all when he shined it directly at her. He moved onto her ears without any real response from

her, either. When he tried to examine her mouth, she opened it wide and gnashed her tiny teeth at him. As soon as his hands were away, she closed her mouth again. The empty look never left her eyes.

The doctor continued his attempts to examine her mouth for a few minutes, without any real progress being made. She hadn't fought with him about her ears or her eyes, and he didn't understand why the mouth was such a strong boundary for her. Finally, he stepped aside and let the scientist speak.

"Sir, I think it would be in everyone's best interest if I take the child to my lab. It's clear we won't get any cooperation while she's alive."

The assistant's mouth fell open. "You mean you want to *kill* her? But she's just a child." Even as she said the words, she wasn't sure she believed them.

The mayor spoke up. "Now, now. I'm sure he doesn't mean *kill* her. And surely whatever you'll do to her in the lab is for the interest of the whole city. Right?"

The scientist stammered. "Well, yes. That's the goal of science. Anything she teaches us would be of tremendous value to the whole town." Under his breath, he added, "Probably." The assistant closed her mouth and folded her arms. Whatever this child was, it didn't deserve to be treated like this.

"What if I took her home?" the assistant offered. "She's so small. Surely she shouldn't have to live in a musty old lab." The child's eyes slowly panned over to the woman. If the assistant was being honest with herself, she had always wanted a child — and if the universe refused to give her one of her own, maybe this was a sign she shouldn't be so picky. Cautiously, she walked back toward the child and gently placed a hand on her shoulder. The child blinked.

The men weren't convinced, but they reluctantly agreed. The assistant would raise the child, and would bring her to the lab when requested. None of the men were cut out for raising a small child, anyway, especially not a young girl, and *especially* not one as peculiar as this. The scientist stipulated, however, that the assistant was not to be present during the experiments. Clearly she had already bonded with the child, and in the interest of science, they must preserve objectivity. The woman gave a frustrated sigh, but agreed. At least the child would have a warm bed to come home to, after the experiments were done. Woman and child left the hall together and walked toward her humble home.

No matter what she tried, the assistant couldn't get the child to eat. She tried to demonstrate picking up food and eating it, but the child only blinked. She even tried offering the child a bite from her own fork — the child only blinked. No matter what the woman did, she couldn't get the child to open her mouth as she had for the doctor. Not that she particularly wanted to be bit, but if she could get some food in there, perhaps instincts would kick in and the child would eat something.

No such luck.

Exhausted, the assistant got up from the table. The child stared at her until she motioned for it to get up. She led the child to the couch and pulled out a blanket and pillow. The child only blinked. The assistant grew increasingly frustrated. Why couldn't the universe have given her a normal, human baby? As much as she had yearned for a child, and for as long, somehow this child was worse than no child at all. She went off to her room in silence and cried herself to sleep.

In the morning, everything was different. The assistant awoke to the sound of screeching from her back patio. The sky was an eerie orange, and beyond the shrill noise, the town was silent. She threw on a sweater and followed the sound.

Standing on the porch was the child, as naked as she had been in the fountain, with her face turned toward the sky. Out of her open mouth and eyes was the brightest light the town had ever seen — far brighter than the sun on the hottest day in recorded history. Dread washed over the assistant. This child wasn't a child at all. It was a beacon.

At the very edge of the beam of light, the assistant could only just make out the edge of a large craft. Its real parents were coming.

The First Meeting

Written by Raissa Batra

It was at 9:30 pm when Aditi felt Mia tap on her shoulder. In less than ten minutes, the joy of meeting her German friend for the first time had evaporated into thin air.

Mia had arrived in Mumbai earlier in the day and was staying at the Taj Mahal Palace Hotel. Her parents were going to be away at a banquet, so she had suggested that Aditi spend the evening with her. They had hugged and Aditi had barely followed Mia into her room when they heard what Aditi initially thought was the sound of crackers.

"Did you hear that?" Aditi asked her.

"What?" Mia asked.

Aditi opened the door. "Shooting", "gunmen", "terrorist attack"—these were the words flying in the corridor. She got the picture. She quickly shut the door, locked it, and backed away as if the gunmen were right outside.

What should they do?

"Hide under the bed, now!" Mia told her. She, too, had grasped the situation. She held up the bedsheets and Aditi crawled inside. She followed after she had piled some furniture by the door.

Aditi and Mia had met over a language learning website. Aditi had been learning German and Mia had been learning English. They corrected each other's assignments online and then they just started talking and they became friends (despite an age difference of two years: Aditi being 13 and Mia being 15). And here their first meeting was taking place under a bed, with an attack going on right outside their door.

"So we just stay here? We have to get out of this building!" Aditi shouted. She could hear her heart pounding.

"If we get out we will surely get killed," Mia replied calmly. Her calmness surprised her. Whereas every passing second Aditi was thinking: what if those gunmen came through the door?

For a while, the gunshots continued, but when they stopped, Aditi took out her phone and tried calling her mother. But she couldn't reach her. Mia also tried calling her parents but no such luck. Aditi wanted to something more than just hiding under the bed. But what? The window glass was so thick, and even if they could somehow break it, it was a huge drop.

Aditi folded her hands and started praying. She fought her tears. God. Is God going to help them get out of this situation? Death. It was so near, there seemed no escape. Would they live or not? Then she felt something: hope. Maybe they wouldn't die.

She told Mia: "You know, everyone has to die someday, but I don't want to die right now and not like this. I want to die peacefully, right next to my family." By now her nerves had steadied somewhat.

They lay under the bed in silence. The single thought swirled in her head. She didn't want to die. Again and again, she said it in her mind: that she didn't want to die. But what could she do? She couldn't do anything. Suddenly, her mind was full of regrets: If only she had not had a tiff with her sister that morning. The sister had wanted to borrow her shoes for the day, but Aditi had refused. Now, she just wanted to hear her voice once more. If only she had not skipped dinner with her parents last night and had not gone to her room to finish her history assignment. She had no idea if the entire family would ever meet for dinner again.

"If we could get out, and that is a big if, what are you going to do?" Aditi asked Mia.

"Huh?"

She repeated the question.

"I'll fly back home as soon as possible. And then try to live my life normally. Before I met you, I got angry at my father and said that he didn't spend any time with me. I want to tell him that I was sorry I said that and I love him. I also hope I don't get nightmares. You know, when I was young, I saw this scary man in a fair and I had nightmares for about a week."

Aditi patted her back.

"So, what would you do?" Mia asked.

"Well, I will write about this episode. You know before I got on my flight, I had this really bad feeling about this trip. It was a strange feeling at that time. If I live, I am going to trust my instincts hereafter. I always thought if something like this would happen, I would be so calm and help people. Well, I wasn't exactly calm, was I?"

"Hey, it happens," Mia replied.

No other conversation was possible. No other thought came to her mind, except death. Aditi had always been curious about what happened after death. She would probably know soon enough.

"I'm scared," she told Mia.

The German girl put her arm around her shoulders and squeezed them and said, "Even I am scared."

It was quite suffocating down there and Aditi had begun to sweat. But she didn't tell Mia to remove her arm. It was comforting.

They heard footsteps and moved closer to each other.

Minutes passed by. Aditi wanted to get out. She started humming nervously. "What—" Mia was about to say something, but Aditi put her hand over her mouth. She put a finger on her lips to tell her to be quiet. Someone was trying to open the door.

Who Needs A Helping Hand?

Written by L'oreal Nicole Lee

One day, I was sitting down at a lunch table in Bo's Café. As I began to read my newspaper, I glanced up at a sign being held by an individual. It read: "I need help. If you have a kind heart, please help."

As I read the sign, I began to think what if that were me out there, wouldn't I want someone to help me? I rose from the table and walked outside to where the man was staying and asked him his name. He said, "I'm, I'm John Madison."

"Hi, I'm Jack," I replied.

"It's nice to meet you Jack," he said.

Then I asked, "Would you like to join me for a cup of coffee?" He smiled and nodded yes, and we walked into the café together.

As we entered people, began to stare at us and I kindly told them that there was nothing to stare at, we were just two gentlemen about to enjoy a nice cup of coffee. They smiled in approval and continued eating their meals.

John and I sat for hours talking about how he ended up on the street. He told me that he was not really a poor man, but was on a mission to see how much the people of America cared about the poor. He explained to me that he had been in ten different cities in 5 different states. Out of 50 places, only ten people offered to help him. That included me. He said that this was his last city and it was now time for him to return to his business in NY. He had to figure out how to get more people involved with giving the poor a helping hand.

Then he said to me, "I will put the same offer on the table for you that I did for the

others."

"What is that?" I asked.

"I want you to work for my company, Helping Hand Inc., delivering food and supplies to the needy in your area and getting the word out about poverty here in America. I will pay you ten dollars an hour," he explained.

I thought about it for a moment, then I accepted the offer. "Ok I'll do it, but you don't have to pay me to help out my brethren."

"But I want to," he said.

"Ok can't argue with that," I said with a smile on my face. We shook hands and that was the start of a beautiful friendship. Little did I know how much this experience would change my life.

The next day, I received a phone call from John. He told me that he had booked a flight for me to New York, so I could see the building he purchased for the main headquarters of the mission. He also asked me if I would move to New York to run it. I lived in D.C. and was doing good for myself there. I thought long and hard about the opportunity presented to me and I accepted. I could help twice as many people by teaching and training others to help the needy.

When I arrived, John was waiting at the gate to greet me. We grabbed my bags and headed to the headquarters to start our first mission. When we arrived at the center, I was surprised at how big it was. There was so much to do to get it ready, we had to get right to work. It had 15 spacious rooms with 6 beds in each one for the homeless to sleep and be warm. There were 3 locker room styled bathrooms with 4 showers and sinks in each one for them to stay clean and healthy. We had three large kitchens to cook and feed them in. There were four large pantries full of food and supplies to hand out the community. There was a call center equipped with top notch office supplies and everything else we need to make this mission a success. The executive staff each had their own office and mine was the biggest, next to John's.

We took about three hours to prepare for the crowd that was about to arrive. Around 3:00pm, they began to arrive. We handed out information about jobs and supplies to the people. They were very grateful for what we were doing for them. Some of them even cried because they were so happy that someone cared about their situation and wanted to help. At that moment, I knew my decision to be here was the right one and my calling was to lend a helping hand and give them some hope back.

We finished up around 8:00pm. I went to my hotel feeling proud of what I had done today. I fell to my knees to pray, I still felt that there was something I was not doing and someone that I was not helping. I began to pray and I had a vision. It showed me that there were people unable to come down to the center. I knew what we had to do.

The next day, I got up around 6:30 am to get ready to go down to the center. In the taxi, I began to draw up a plan to get the supplies to those who could not come and get them. I arrived at the center at 7:00 am, very excited about my plan. I presented it to John and the others; they loved it. We found a place to rent large food delivery trucks from until we purchased our own. We fill the truck up with food and supplies. At 9:00am, we left to deliver the food and supplies.

Our first stop was the Bronx. It was rough to see how these people were living. Their windows had bars or boards covering them up, people were being evicted from their homes, and many slept outside on park benches. Tears ran down my cheek as I looked on. We finally stopped in front of a rundown apartment building where a crowd awaited us as if they knew we were coming. As we hopped out of the truck, we were greeted by many with hugs and kisses. We walked to the back of the truck and opened it. The people gathered around the truck to see what was inside. We began handing out the food and supply packages. As we continued to do so, I was approached by a woman. She told me that there was an older lady unable to leave her apartment and needed someone to bring her packages up to her.

I grabbed the biggest package of food we had on the truck and made my way to the building. As I was approaching the building, I noticed a group of gang bangers staying in the hallway. I took a deep breath and entered the building, they immediately stopped me in my tracks. I was scared but ready to defend myself. I had learned how to hold my own growing up in DC. Their sergeant walked up to me, "Hi man, this is a real cool thing you are doing for my hood, you welcome around here anytime."

I said, "Thanks man," and he stepped to the side to let me pass.

I was glad that this building had an elevator because she lived on the 12th floor. As the elevator began to move, I thought about how relieved I was that I didn't have to fight. I realized that this was the beginning of something new that would make a difference in my life and many others. The elevator stopped and the doors opened. I stepped into the hallway. It reeked of piss, blacks, and weed. There was dirt and trash everywhere. I walked down the hall, watching my step, until I reached apartment 1222. I knocked on the door, and a sweet, soft, little voice answered, "Come in, suga."

I opened the door and walked in. "Hello ma'am, how are you today?" I asked.

"I'm just fine, and you?" she said with a smile.

Just then her daughter walked in, looking like she was heaven sent. "Hey momma," she said.

"Hey honey…" the old lady replied. "This is… is…what's your name, suga?"

"Oh, my name is Jack, I'm part of Helping Hand Inc." I replied.

"Hi, I'm Jessica," she said with a smile.

"Nice to meet you, Jessica…" I said as I placed the package on the table to shake her hand. "Oh and I will go grab your other packages, ma'am."

"Oh call me Mrs. Smith…" she said. "And Jessica why don't you go down and help this nice handsome gentleman with those packages?"

"Yes ma'am, momma," Jessica replied.

I opened the door for her and we walked out into the hallway to get on the elevator. As we rode down, I thought about how beautiful she was and if she had a boyfriend. We reached the first floor and walked outside toward the truck. As we were walking she started asking me how I got involved with Helping Hand Inc. While we grabbed the packages off the truck, I told her all about how I met John and the offer he made me. She seemed very interested in hearing more about the program and me.

We took the packages and headed back toward the building. As we got on the elevator to go back upstairs, she asked me if I would like to have dinner with her after work. I said "YES" with no hesitation. We reached the apartment and as we entered, her mother was sitting in her rocking chair, grinning from ear to ear. We placed the packages down on the counter and exchanged numbers.

As I headed towards the door, her mother said, "You all enjoy your dinner tonight." I stopped and turn to look at Jessica, but she was already looking at me with the same expression on her face. How did she know about our date tonight? She saw the expressions on our faces and said, "Momma knows everything that goes on with her children," as she continued rocking and grinning. I told Jessica I would be back to pick her up at 7:30pm and left.

As John and I finished handing out the packages, I told him all about Jessica. He said that he was glad I found something else to keep me busy other than work. We went back to the center. When we got there, I started finishing up my paperwork, so I could leave to get ready for my date with Jessica. On my way out the door, John stopped me, "Hi, I know you're not going to pick her up in a taxi."

"But I don't have a car," I said.

"Well you do now," John said as he handed me a set of keys to a new Lexus.

"Thanks John, I'm going to pay you back," I said.

"Don't worry about it, think of it as your first bonus," he said as he walked away.

I walked outside to the parking lot to see my new whip; it was fly. I hopped in and headed for my hotel to get dressed.

I arrived at Jessica's Apartment at 7:30pm. I called her to let her know I was downstairs. I parked the car and walked to the building to meet her. When she stepped off the elevator, it was like I heard angels sing in the background; she was stunning.

"You look beautiful," finally flew out my mouth.

"Thank you," she said with a smile. We walked back to the car and I opened her door for her and let her climb inside. Then I closed it and walked around to the driver's side and got in. I turned on the radio and as I pulled off one of her favorite songs came on the radio, "Happily Ever After" by Case.

We drove to the Upper Eastside to this nice little club. We arrived there and were escorted inside to a nice table. We sat down to look at the dinner menu. The club was nice. It had a bar, dance floor, VIP rooms, and a spacious dining area to eat. The waiter came over to take our order. After we were done ordering, we began talking more about me and the program. Just then "Too Close" by Next came bumping through the speakers.

"Let's dance," she said as she grabbed my hand and led me to the dance floor. We started dancing; she was a decent dancer. We danced to the next couple of songs and then sat down to eat.

"You're a nice dancer," she said.

"You're not too bad yourself" I told her.

For a moment, we just sat and stared until the waiter asked, "Will that be all?"

"Oh yeah man, we good, thank you," I answered.

We ate and enjoyed one another's company. After we finished eating and had dessert, we left. We drove around for about an hour just looking at the lights of the city. After driving around, we went to Putt-Putt. I let her win the game. As I drove her home, we listened to music and laughed. We said goodnight and I went home.

The next morning, she met me down at the center. Jessica was going to help us deliver packages. We first began Uptown at about 9 am. We visited the Davidsons first, they were rude to us but took the packages anyway. Next, we visited the Garysons family. They were a nice family, they even made us some brownies. We made a few more stops, then headed to Manhattan. The people in Manhattan were a lot more friendly and we finished our route in no time.

We got back to the center around 3pm. We put the extra food and supplies away and completed the paperwork. Afterwards, me and Jessica went to have dinner. I was really feeling her, and she was feeling me. We spent many evenings together and, in due time, we fell in love.

The program lasted for years and was a great success. Me and Jessica got engaged and were soon married. We are still happily married after 20 years. We have two wonderful children in college. I received a citizenship award for my effort to put a dent in the population of starving people in New York. I am now retired, but occasionally we still visit the center and help. When my children are home from college they also help at the center. They have made plans to open centers where they go to school.

A New Kind of Virus

Written by Carrington Parrott

It has been over a year since the start of the changing; the world is a wasteland in most parts and the graves are piled high. Exactly what the movies had shown was what had happened, a virus that changes the brain and effectively makes you a "zombie". We just call them The Fallen, it makes it easier to put them to rest. I am part of a small group that crossed the country in search of a safe location to begin building our new safe haven. I knew Mercury before this all began, met him while he toured with his little hometown band, hence his unique name. I go by Iris, have ever since I went on the road with him and started a new life being his touring girl. We have five others in our post-apocalyptic family:

Shay, the mother figure we all needed. She is well in her thirties and doesn't take shit from anyone else, a true spitfire of a woman. She has been the brains of our group and often the brawn as well.

Frank is older than Shay and a profoundly serious guy. I am not sure if even Shay knows too much about him, but he's her right-hand man. He keeps us alive with his knowledge of survival and common sense.

Grace we picked up somewhere between leaving Dallas and arriving in Oklahoma. She is a thirteen-year-old kid who watched her family become infected, watched as strangers killed all of them, and was hiding in fear that they would come back to finish her off. She is like our post-apocalyptic daughter, her hair always braided and her laugh always chiming in at the oddest of times. She could find the good in almost anything and that was something we had all come to rely on heavily.

Allen and Brie we found together, same as Mercury and I. Allen is eighteen and Brie almost nineteen. Brie's is the bubbliest person you'll ever meet, and her blonde hair is so light it will blind you. Allen is a dorky guy, smart as hell and sometimes a little too honest; he reminds me of my brother.

Mercury is a typical tall and handsome type. He and I are twenty-four, heavily tattooed, and only soft for each other. Yeah, the typical teenage love story that just never really grew out of that "phase". Mercury used to be a pretty quiet guy, but with our group he likes to talk to fill the time now.

We have one truck for our travels. Shay drives with Frank shotgun; only Grace gets to sit inside the cab with our belongings and food we have scavenged. The rest of us bide our time in the bed of the truck, blankets and jackets to hide from the sun on our often long journeys from decaying town to fallen city. We have not seen a Fallen person in many months. Once the world figured out that death was the only cure, we have been careful to not let anyone make it into the final stage of the virus. It is a harsh way to run things but, if you get ill, you get killed. It saves all of us in the long run.

We made it up into the old state of New York, upstate New York that is, and it has been a decent stay. Well, except for Grace developing a cough.

"Drink some water." I tell her when her coughing fit lasts a few seconds too long for comfort.

Grace nods, unable to fully speak. She gulps down half her water bottle and wipes her mouth with the back of her hand. "It's probably just the dirt and sand."

I nod, unconvinced, an all too familiar sadness falling over me. I look to Mercury who is in the midst of a debate with Allen, his lip ring gleaming in the sun with every word he speaks. Allen's curly brown hair bouncing around as he passionately refutes whatever Mercury says. I've grown to love our misfit family.

Shay determines an abandoned house is safe for us to stay in. We all unload the truck and bring our few belongings inside. The house hasn't been too messed with, family pictures still line the walls, it feels as if we are in a museum. We claim bedrooms, board windows to aid against other people who might attempt to rob the place while we stay here. Some people took the new way of life to the extreme and they do not mind killing those of us who they come across.

I find a box in the kitchen, a little safety deposit box the previous owners must have used. I almost just leave it alone, but there's writing on the side. "IMPORTANT INFORMATION INSIDE." I curse myself for being so nosy and I take the box into mine and Mercury's room. I will find no method of opening it for days on end.

Grace finds the keys to the house while exploring and adds them to her weird collection of, yes, keys. She has been collecting them since we took her in' I think she gets a satisfying feeling of hope from them. We let her do it, it doesn't hurt the group in any way.

We spend our time in this house sleeping and playing Yahtzee over and over since it seems to be the only board game in the place. Shay and I run some trips to the little downtown of this city and scavenge for food and other useful resources. A week after arriving at this stop, Grace's symptoms worsen. She coughs more frequently; she has a low-grade fever and gets cold sweats randomly. I already know where this illness is headed, and I am sure Shay does too.

The defining symptom occurred two weeks into our stop. Grace is rolling the dice during a game and her nose begins to bleed. We all fall silent, I look to Shay and she is already looking back at me. Frank must already know some plan through Shay because he gets Allen and Brie to go outside with him for some random task. I go with Shay to another area of the house and Mercury watches Grace, laughing and keeping her calm.

"We saw this coming." I tell Shay as we step across the threshold of the kitchen.

She sighs and her body language is something I have never seen from her before. She looks defeated. "I don't know that I can do this one." I know what she means, and I know what she is asking of me.

I nod, solemn and quiet. We stand there for a while and just hate our new world for what it makes us do. Eventually I get up the courage to move and Shay gives me a last look before I return to where Mercury and Grace are still playing the board game.

"Grace, I think you should rest." She looks over to me, not a hint of sadness detectable on my face, for I don't want to scare her.

She rolls the dice one last time, actually winning the game. She looks up to me, her face is droopy with lack of energy and she agrees to go try and nap.

I walk with her to her room and she looks up to me. "I want

to show you a key." She's so tired as she says this, but she digs through her backpack anyways. I give her a couple of minutes, but she never finds the new key she is so excited about. "I'll show you when I get up," she decides.

She gets into bed and I read her part of a book I found a few stops back in Tennessee. It's been a routine that her and I have had for a while. It is not long before her eyes flutter shut, and her breathing pattern relaxes. She is asleep and my heart sinks to my stomach.

Careful not to wake her, I lift an extra pillow from beside her, covering her young, beautiful face. Her two braids peeking out from underneath the pile of fabric I am holding down forcefully. A lump forms in my throat as she is awakened by her body's need for air, I close my eyes and ride out the fight. I finally put her to rest. She was too many stages into the virus to allow her to remain with us. She would have soon become contagious, and not long after that stage she would be Fallen. I stop that from happening and I cry in Mercury's arms all night.

A week later and I cannot stand to remain in this house anymore. The boys have buried Grace out in the backyard respectfully and I cannot bear to look at her little grave. I see her in every room of this place. We all pack our things into the truck, an empty spot left in the back bench of the cab. I return to the house to get Grace's things, as I pick up her backpack a key is underneath. It belongs to a lockbox; the shape is unmistakable. My heart skips a beat as I remember the box I had left under my bed. With great sadness, I make my way back to its hiding spot.

The key works, the metal top pops open and I see journal entries inside. I find the first one and begin there.

If you are reading this then you have survived the virus long enough to see all of the stages...or so you thought. Four months ago, I discovered that the virus no longer reaches the stage of completion. Patients are no longer becoming living dead. I have many records in my journal, all of them proving my discovery. I will be making my way to the CDC to hopefully get the message out to the entire world. We do not need to kill the ill anymore, we have not needed to for quite a while. Please, if you find this, spread the word.

I am numb upon reading these words. I cannot change the present nor right the wrongs of my past. Shay enters the room behind me. I do not respond to her questions and she eventually pulls the letter from my hand. I barely hear her cry out; I barely hear anything at all. A new kind of virus is washing over me, and it is not the one we have been running from, but instead it is one that we have created all on our own. I am distraught inside and I now feel this empty pit grow within myself and it feels as large as the hole in which Grace lies.

If she had just found that key...

School Day

Written by Milo Cumaranatunge

We packed into the backseat of the turquoise Austin Mini, family friend Ajit, my brother and I, and headed to St. Richard's prep school for boys, a private school and unusual for Sri Lanka, but not uncommon in the capital city of Colombo. We had St. Joseph's, St. Peter's, St. Benedict's, and so on, all spread out in a city of one million people. But my little school stood alone next to the beach, although now when I think back, I never noticed the sea. Swaying through traffic, amongst a cacophony of car horns, noise from broken tail pipes, and road rage, and breathing in air full of fumes from burning engine oil, melting rubber, and the occasional garbage dump on the street, the three of us would insulate the inside of our car with song.

Every day we would sing through the entire car ride, starting with the school anthem and ending with our favorite Rugby song, a limerick, into which you could insert any girl's name for an edge. We always used Ajit's sister's name. She sat in front, going to her school, St. Mary's Convent, another school named after a saint, but for girls. She never smiled and would threaten to tell on us to her father, which would alarm us until

Ajit dismissed it with a nonchalant shake of his head. The song, not really vulgar or crude, essentially translated into how somebody brought some fish for this girl with a great behind. In retrospect, it made little sense, but no one cared back then, except for maybe Ajit's sister.

We were of that age where we wanted to be close to girls, but didn't know why. Like most days, we arrived at school late, and the day started with a rush. At the assembly, where the multi-ethnic plural society of Sri Lanka split into their respective religions for an hour, we Buddhists went to the main hall while the Christians went to Chapel. They had a special place, being this was an Anglican missionary school founded by the British – our colonial forefathers, now long departed. Their schools cherished tradition above all, including wearing long pants and blazers to school in the scorching island sun. I parroted through the first part of chanting at Buddhist assembly, and got collared for talking during the second part by a Prefect – an older student leader.

He admonished me to be silent. As always, I threatened back with silence, and a solemn vow to become Head Prefect one day. As grandiose thoughts of preparing the duty roster for the Prefects as the school Head Prefect streamed through my mind, I also noted I had just eight years to go and needed to prove my worthiness of such an honor, bestowed on the most exceptional students. Class always started slowly, usually with a period - hour long session - of language instruction.

Sri Lanka had three official languages, and, to my chagrin, we studied all three. I paid little attention except for math and science. During math class, the teacher, a tall lanky fellow with a bad temper, tried something new. He recited a problem and asked any student who solved it to call out the answer. As luck would have it, my voice rang out first, three times out of

Five. There were some 'brainiacs' in the class, but I had never seen myself as one.

The social studies teacher did not show up. I started one of my favorite activities in school, recounting the story of a recent movie I had been allowed to see by my liberal parents. My audience, kids from all over the country who called the school lodging house home - boarders, we called them - appreciated my every word. Today's story, "Blood Money," a movie from Hong Kong full of Kung Fu, appealed to our young minds.

Coupled with my embellishments accompanied by abrupt hand motions, the story episodes would drag on for months, but my faithful listeners never faltered. By fifth period, all of us waited for recess, or "interval," as the Commonwealth – ex-British colonies – called it. Recess time meant soccer, the great premier league tournament where two teams, more like gangs of soccer players, played each other every school day for dominance and bragging rights. Two influential classmates led each team, but they were not great speakers, or movers, or shakers. They just had parents who were rich enough, or were inattentive enough, to give their sons adequate pocket money to spend on their friends at the school tuck shop. I was not a leader, but I was one of the great soccer players of our time, currying favors from the best of them to be recruited to the team most likely to win.

Wilson, the peon at the school office and the oldest employee of the school who also, poor man, happened to have a bum leg, rang the ten-pound recess bell by hand. The second we heard the bell, our class sent out runners tasked with the mission to capture the prize goalposts before anyone else. Inevitably, older students would hijack our playing area or simply play their game on the same field as ours. Sometimes, there could be up to five games of soccer being played on the same field at the same time, an amazing sight to see. Every game was wracked with incidents where an outsider would accidentally contribute towards scoring or saving a goal in your game.

I frequently arrived late and my team would hold the kickoff, sparking an early disagreement that would occasionally build on others to eventually result in all-out brawls by the end of the game. Once the game started, I hung out close to the opponent's goal waiting for an opening; after all, the best soccer players are opportunists, getting to the right place at the right time. And any attempt to enforce the offside rule was sheer lunacy. The entire student body wore the same uniforms. Sometimes visibility would drop to a few feet by the dust kicked up from the sandy field where a blade of grass was rare as a referee's whistle. Those grounds had little chance of turning green after being stomped on by a thousand little feet on a daily basis.

But the biggest trick during play was staying alive. The game was dangerous, with errant soccer balls flying across your face and the real possibility of getting stampeded by one of the older bigger boys, especially Hettiarachchi or Bartholomew, hulking monsters roaming the arena, reminiscent of Kaiju, giant beasts from Japanese cartoons. Hettiarachchi, Hetts for short since Sri Lankans have the longest surnames, was easier to avoid, being he rolled along like a barrel of oil.

Bartholomew, on the other hand, known as Batha to anyone who had the misfortune of meeting him on the field of play, was ripped to the core, and he moved with the power and grace of an albino impala navigating the African bush. I recall being thrown from bumping into Batha and him reaching out and scooping me inches off the ground before I cracked my skull.

After planting me back on my feet, he said something in broken Sinhala, the most widely spoken language in the country, and ran off chasing his ball again. His incomprehensible verse was no apology; it was closer to "Get the hell out of my track." I supposed English was his preferred language considering he descended from Dutch Burghers, another ex-colonial master, now forming another ethnic group in our country.

Nothing came my way for ten minutes when somebody kicked our ball over the wall separating the school grounds from the rail track running along the beach. Every year that wall lost a few inches to the elements. The salty air had stripped away the mortar and created diverts – perfect footholds for a ten-year-old. And the railroad didn't look any better. The British had built a rail line circumnavigating our island like a rope holding the country together. Like many conquerors – the Romans built roads – the British built railroads as a means to project their power.

As Sri Lanka had not built a new rail line since the British left, I assumed they were a hundred years old. We rushed the suspect who kicked the ball into the forbidden zone, but backed down, realizing it was an older boy of smaller stature. Gathering at the boundary between official school property and land belonging to the state – no private beachfront ownership in Sri Lanka – we vented at the randomness of our game and the consequential delay. The rail track was deemed too dangerous for students under the age of fourteen. Protocol dictated we wait for a Perfect to get the ball. But the leader of our team, Aziz – I never knew where he went for assembly – jumped over the wall to get the ball.

The wall separating our field of melee from the thundering diesel engines and carriages barreling across the tracks was not a wall, but more like a rabbit-proof fence. Aziz, a man with a mission, rose to the occasion. Just before he threw the ball back over, the captain of our team placed some hand-sized granite rocks right on the rails of the track. We had heard this done before, resulting in spectacular mini-explosions when the iron wheels of the locomotives ran over them. We promptly stopped the game awaiting the next train. But the jig was up.

A Prefect spotted us and another one hundred or so kids saw our intrepid leader's handiwork as well. Within minutes, the Prefects hauled us into the Headmaster's office, a room paneled in wood showing all the names of every Headmaster and Head Prefect since 1886, and a large desk holding center stage. The Headmaster, Mr. J.S.L. Pereira – Jerald Shelly Lionel, used by us in another rugby song – sat in his chair listening to the Prefect explain Aziz's crime. The old man rose from his desk, exposing the baggiest of white trousers and told us to leave except for the culprit. As we stood outside, the sound of the cane ripping through the air and striking raw flesh imprinted into my brain like the Ten Commandments. Ten times it still rings out, as though Gutenberg himself had done the printing.

When we walked back into the office, to my surprise, Aziz was not crying. Actually, I would say he sported a slight smile tending to his welts. The man wore his battle scars with pride. The headmaster began to question why a young boy would commit such a dastardly act.

As the Prefects looked at each other, I raised my hand. To this day I don't know why or how it happened, but I said, "Sir, I think we need a better barrier. The wall only encourages students to jump over it."

With all eyes on me, J.S.L. nodded and focused on me over his spectacles, wearing an expression I deciphered as, "Think I know this kid's father," which in those days meant an express ticket to the top. Then he said, "I say young man! Speak up!"

Seizing the opportunity to make my mark on enhancing the recess experience and the Headmaster's opinion of a certain fourth grader, I said, "We should have a Prefect on duty at the wall during interval, sir!"

"Don't we have one already?" the Headmaster said, eying the Prefects once again. The poor 12th-grade student leaders looked like puppets, turning their heads at each other unable to speak. "I say... very bad show. Call the Head Prefect," the Headmaster said, his lower lip quivering, and turning the edges of his mouth down he nodded at me, which I interpreted as "Good job son."

Walking back to class, Aziz and I were the solitary ones smiling. Aziz had sealed my
loyalty to his team for the rest of my illustrious career, and I had taken my first steps toward the goal of becoming Head Prefect by seizing the Headmaster's eye.

The Window

Written by Adam Silver

As I gaze out my window, I'm an adult, surrounded by faceless, gleaming glass office towers and condos on top of one another. The sky is a clear blue on a crisp, but comfortable, spring day. Outside it is eerily quiet, not even the sound of a bird chirping; all I can hear is the occasional rumble of an 18-wheeler making a delivery next door. The air smells fresh on this day, a relief from the stale air of a cold winter. As I gaze upon my room, I feel as if I'm the only soul around in a prison of my own making.

It wasn't always this way. I remember looking through a different window, and suddenly, I'm transported back to the Midwood section of Brooklyn, the place of my birth. I am 7 years old and have witnessed a lunar landing, and, though I don't know it yet, the Amazin' Mets are about to make a miracle that will be even more monumental than the first man landing on the moon. The view is different, as well; there are cars parked all along the one-way street, there are people outside walking and playing, as I will be in a moment, and neighbors sitting down together and chatting at their stoops and porches.

I race out of my home, knowing that I won't have to return

until the street lights turn on, and, as this is the Summer of 1969, that means I can stay out way late, probably past 8pm. I run into my pal Tony, who I admire because he is the richest kid on the block (when he and his younger brother Francis would get into fights, which was often, you knew because their mom would have them wear a frozen steak on their eyes; the rest of us just had to use ice). Oh, the games we'd play passed down from generations of Brooklynites we would never know, games whose rules weren't written, but etched in your memory, and disputes would be resolved, and if they couldn't, everyone was agreeable to a do-over. We made use of the physical surroundings, such as the wide and high stoops for stoop ball, the street for stickball, with the parked cars as

bases (and if someone stoked a Spaulding so hard that it smashed a window, we'd get some extra running in), and then the sidewalk for my personal favorite, skelly, where I learned the art of flicking your wrist with a bottle cap. Those were the days.

It wasn't always like that either. About one year after the Miracle, my family was uprooted to some faraway place called Long Island. I would gaze out of my window sulking, hoping that my misery would convince my parents to return to Brooklyn where I was happy. The view outside was like a desert, not a soul outside besides my sisters and myself; the street I lived on had very few kids my age. Neighbors had huge fences built between their properties, so there was no chance of sitting down and chatting on a nonexistent stoop, or even porches, which did exist. Not a single car parked on the street, rather here people parked in garages. Occasionally, I'd hear the sounds of birds chirping and singing on the tree-lined street, but other than that, there was silence. I had this eerie feeling that over time, I was the only soul around in a prison of my own making.

My plan to be so miserable that the family would be forced to move back to Brooklyn never did pan out. It was a fantasy of mine that I kept going for many years, likely too long. I never attempted to make the best of it in my new surroundings and I turned inward. A happy boy was now quiet and fearful, especially around other people. It became a template of my life.

The large, glassy towers that line my view resemble towers housing prison guards. The only difference is that the occupants of these dull glass buildings can leave; my internal prison forces me to stay put. Flashbacks in my life take up the scenery, and I imagine getting a second chance at some decisions I made. I'm a young adult with a small group of friends who felt stagnated by their refusals to do anything different than spending nights getting drunk in a dive bar that had roaches as pets. My decision to walk away from my friends was based on the notion

that I would be able to connect somehow with friends I made at college. However, the new circle of close friends never materialized as I had hoped; we remained friends, but only when college was in session. I look at the many dates I had but never pursued. The one woman that keeps getting into my head from time to time was someone who made it obvious to me that she wanted more than a platonic friendship. My anxiety derailed any thought of any personal relationship developing. When college ended, so did any close personal contact.

Looking out the window, I realize this is my destiny, and it all goes back to that miserable eight-year-old who longed to return to his birthplace. He was too young and innocent to understand any better, now as an adult, I realize we have to live with the choices we make. There can be no plan to go back from where you came. There's no chance of getting a second opportunity to reverse decisions you made. These are the consequences of life. You know, I don't think I'm the only one that lives in a prison of his own making.

The Last Supper

Written by L. Player

Her tears; they fall like limp dead bodies. They caress my sweater and drop onto the seat, leaving circular watermarks. I lift up her shirt and tell her that it'll be okay. When she says that she doesn't believe me, I don't say anything, because even I don't believe me. This isn't the time nor place to cause a scene, but when time ceases to exist, and the only place you want to visit says you must leave, all logic goes out the door. I tell her that it's not her fault, that it was a mistake, that we can go to another pet store. None of this matters because a few hours later when we are on the news, we have lost all chances of ever visiting another store again.

•

Toni attempts to adjust her seat quietly, but fails in doing so. The legs of the chair scraping against the floor has alarmed us all. I squint at her, and she smiles. No matter what I do, she'll laugh. I tell her *I know* when she calls me funny. Every word that escapes her tongue is filled with pure intent. Rather than pretending as though everything she wants to say is "good," she's always blunt. Her explanations leave me soothed, as though when giving a speech to a crowd, she'd calm us all. The rug under my bed is left untouched as I prefer to prostrate in front of her.

Last week we received a special surprise at home; the mailwoman accidentally left the dog pamphlet on our doorstep. Toni showed it to me, her fingers pointing to the "Dog Training" section. I tell her, "This isn't very intentional of you," but naturally, we agree to attend a session. It takes her hours to dress because she believes the occasion is a once in a lifetime experience. Her outfit cannot be anything less than perfect but when she exits the bedroom, I wonder what she's done. On her feet are the Jordans I recently bought her: the ones with the *white* bottom. When I say, "You look sexy," as I focus my attention on her naked stomach, she gives me that look. It's the raise of the eyebrow, the pose, the hand on her hip: this is her mannerism when she's about to read my mind. Her bottom lip curves upwards into a smile when I question why she's cut her "That's what she said!" shirt in half. Her silence carries its way into the car and conceals my disbelief long after I cover her belly in hickeys.

On the drive there, we play a heart chakra Tibetan bowl CD. I yell, "Om" as loud as possible, and then she yells at me to shut up. When the second "Om" plays she screams along with her head out the window. This is a cancer sun sign in rare action. I know that she'll crawl back into her safe space soon, somewhere far from where I am. But for now, she slaps her turtle stickers on my legs and when I tell her to quit playing, she won't listen. In a quick instance, I slightly swerve into another lane amidst avoiding her attacks. Her laugh is so loud that it travels into the car we nearly hit and eases the fear that the "Baby on Board" sticker causes. This is nothing to us, for a little bit of death is sometimes all that we need.

By the time we pull up to the parking lot she gracefully runs in front of me. Her eyes set on the prize, she fills her basket with dog treats in hopes of pleasing them all. One hand is at her side, the other extended to pet every dog. I can't seem to get tired of her saying "Aww" as she scratches their chins. Her dimples leave imprints on my soul, imprints on my cheek, engraving forever marks of joy. When the ugliest dog of them all poops by us and leaves stains on her sneakers, it's then that the white bottoms turn to brown bottoms. Her laugh ripples through the air like a whirlpool, leaving an aftertaste of disbelief on the back of my tongue. She reassures me that she can wipe off the shit with a napkin and when she dangles the cleaned shoe in my face, I believe her. She finds a way to divert my anger elsewhere by pointing out the little things such as the senior boxer who won't quit farting. So naturally, when the dog trainer steps to us, I expect him to tell us we should get a dog but instead, he says that we're being disruptive and if we continue to be, we'll be escorted out. Toni asks the dog trainer, "What?" and when the trainer repeats himself word for word, she looks at me. In a few seconds, I tell him why it's crucial for us to stay. The other people begin to stare, and their whispers cloud my head. I can't imagine what they're thinking and how they possibly can't understand. The trainer tells me he won't argue with me and forces us to leave.

•

I lay with Toni in the back of the car. When we finish, we embrace one another and from the window I watch her tears fall like the dead bodies. These bodies attempt to escape the flames that consume them but fail in doing so. They run as though they know pain, but they don't know pain like watching Toni hurt because if they did, they wouldn't be on fire.

The Swoozlemunger

Written by Michael Frank Rohr

Zsofia the Monster Hunter was off on another great adventure. Chief Noogala of Nippateetee island had sent his trusty king parrot to ask her if she could catch the dreaded Swoozlemunger for his village.

Zsofia was not some ordinary girl—she had an amazing talent for hunting monsters. On a hunt, she always wore her light green overalls, brown leather boots, trusty backpack, and wide brim jungle hat over her golden blonde hair. Chief Noogala had heard stories of her famous adventures, including the slimy Shagglefink of Scaramunge Forest, a slippery, slimy monster with the body of a slug, two heads, and a stinger in its tail.

There was also the Crabblehopper of the Seven Mystery Caves, a huge crab-like creature with large, hairy nippers and legs like a kangaroo.

And, of course, her last hunt, the Bingabobber of Gobble Desert, a slithering snake with a frilly neck and shark fins all down its spine.

Poobo, the chief's prize king parrot held out his foot to show Zsofia the message scroll. As Zsofia unrolled it, Poobo squawked out the message:

"Dear Zsofia, please come quick, the Swoozlemunger is running amok. It's eating our fish and scaring our kids, we are not having any luck. It's making the villagers scream and shout and all we have left are brussel sprouts."

The village children were having horrible nightmares about brussel sprouts. Have you ever had brussel sprouts on toast? Well, now you know why this was such a problem. Something had to be done. It was up to our brave hero Zsofia the Monster Hunter to catch the beast.

Zsofia arrived on Nippateetee Island to a huge party thrown by the chief. The village cook had made the largest brussel sprout cake with brussels icing and sprout sprinkles to thank her for coming. That night the loud, gassy sounds coming from under the villagers' sheets gave Zsofia horrible, smelly nightmares!

The next morning, Zsofia strapped on her trusty monster hunting backpack, which had her super-duper monster spotting glasses, her handheld, infrared, radioscopic, and magnetismo monster finder 3000, also known as the HIRM 3000, which she had designed herself. She packed her fantastic, springlastic, triple-weave monster hunting rope, some spare socks, and a can of baked beans, as she would turn green at the sight of another brussel sprout.

Zsofia found the best spot on the island to begin her hunt. She turned on the HIRM 3000 and walked around Nippateetee all morning but found nothing. She was just about to break for a baked bean lunch and change out of her smelly, sweaty socks when the HIRM 3000 started beeping loudly! BEEP, BEEP, BEEP, BEEP, BEEP. Finally, she had a clue as to where the Swoozlemunger might be hiding.

The signal led her down to a dark hidden sea cave, far from

the village. She decided to put on her super-duper monster spotting glasses. Zsofia climbed slowly down the sharp rock face and poked her head around the corner into the mouth of the scary cave.

With her trusty monster spotting glasses, she saw a huge shape at the back of the cave. All of a sudden, she heard a loud SNORE, burp, burp, SNORE, burp, burp come out of the cave. *The dreaded Swoozlemunger must be sleeping, and boy does he stink of fish*, Zsofia thought as she held her breath.

She decided to lay a trap for the beast at the mouth of the cave with her fantastic, springlastic, triple-weave monster hunting rope. No monster had ever escaped from it, not even the slimy Shagglefink of Scaramunge Forest, which was so slippery and slimy even giant banana slugs were disgusted by it.

Zsofia quickly set her trap and headed back to the village to change out of her smelly, sweaty socks. *Her feet would probably be smelling as bad as the Swoozlemungers breath by now*, she thought.

She was very tired and knew it would be a while before the Swoozlemunger would wake up, and she would need her strength when she returned the next morning. The only thing she had to figure out now was how to avoid the next helping of brussel sprouts from the village cook!

That afternoon, the villagers were amazed to find their morning catch of fish untouched by the Swoozlemunger. "The fantastic, springlastic, triple-weave monster hunting rope trap must have trapped the Swoozlemunger!" The chief shouted. He could hardly believe his eyes and ordered a mighty celebration.

Zsofia walked back to the cave the next morning to find the beast caught in her trap, crying! It sobbed, "Who are you, and why would want to trap a nice Swoozlemunger like me?"

Zsofia proudly said, "My name is Zsofia, the greatest monster hunter in the world, and you are a fish thief."

"Fish thief – that's not right. The local villagers steal *my* fish," the Swoozlemunger cried.

Zsofia was confused. "But Chief Noogala told me that, every day, you eat their catch of fish and terrify the villagers, not to mention mess up their tablecloths."

The Swoozlemunger looked ashamed. "Yes, I have done that, but each night at midnight, I swim out to the deep reef to chase the biggest fish back toward the shallow waters of Nippateetee island; this makes them easy to catch the next day after my morning nap," he said. "By the time I wake up, ready for my fish feast, the villagers have already caught all the best fish. It's not fair! That's why I go to the village. Also, brussel sprouts give me gas."

After hearing the Swoozlemunger's story, Zsofia decided to free him from her fantastic, springlastic, triple-weave monster hunting rope, as long as he agreed to never steal fish from the village again. The Swoozlemunger had no choice but to say, "I *promise*."

In return, Zsofia said sorry for trapping him and set him free. "Stay right here and go out tonight as normal, tomorrow will be different, I promise," she said. Zsofia waved goodbye and walked back to the village to tell the Chief the Swoozlemungers story. After hearing the story, chief Noogala told Zsofia the fishermen had come back to shore with empty nets that morning, which meant the Smoozlemunger was telling the truth. "The Swoozlemunger was not so terrible after all," said Chief Noogala, and he thought to himself it was his duty to come up with a plan to fix everything.

Next morning, the fishermen had in their nets the best catch of fish all year, thanks to the Swoozlemunger.

After his morning nap, the Swoozlemunger woke to find a huge, tasty pile of fish at the entrance of his cave. He was so excited to see the villagers had picked the biggest, juiciest fish and kindly shared them with him as a thank you. They left a note, inviting him to a fire dance feast and named him "Swoozlemunger the Great," protector of Nippateetee Island.

Later that night, Nippateetee was filled with music, dancing, laughter, and there was not a brussel sprout to be seen! After the party Zsofia was in a rush, as she was off on her next great monster hunting adventure! She said goodbye to the villagers, the Swoozlemunger, and Chief Noogala, but did not know about the brussel sprout cookies the Chief had secretly put in her backpack as a surprise snack on her trip home. Stay tuned for Zsofia the Monster Hunter's next great adventure!

Lucky Seven

Written by Claire A Murray

I was never lucky. Made one bad decision after another. Then, an unlucky roll of the dice left this Nebraska farm gal stranded in Vegas, owing Nicky Stones a bundle. Last week he warned me to leave Vegas. I didn't listen.

The blackjack tables didn't entice me, although plenty of other dames sidled up to the tuxedoed players. Craps, that's my game. Those tables were hoppin'. I smoothed my gown and hustled over. Watched how the dice were running.

In craps, winning and losing numbers depend on where you are in the game. Roll seven or eleven in phase one—the Come Out roll—Pass bets win; Don't, Pass bets lose. Roll either one in phase two—after Point is set— Pass bets lose; Don't, Pass bets win. Sounds confusing, but this gal has a brain for numbers, rules, and betting combinations.

I dug into the pocket of my evening bag. The one chip I'd managed to save slid into my fingers and I set that thousand-dollar orange chip on Pass, praying Nicky's table crew didn't recognize me, hair newly dyed blond, bright red lipstick—no Nebraska here.

"Seven." The stickman pulled the dice back. I'd doubled

my money. And my heart rate. I fanned myself and added my win—another orange chip—to my original. Shooter rolled again. "Four. Point." Phase two began, with the shooter needing to roll another four to win. He won that round, but not the next. I'd bet against him and won. New game. The player to his left became the shooter.

Evening slithered into night. Shooters and players came and went. The bright lights glittering off sequins, lighters, and metal fixtures tricked one's senses with the false aura of daytime. I changed my bets, reading players and dice like never before. Noise and the crowd at the table grew, along with my winnings. I grabbed a drink and shut out all but the table. The dice went to the player on my right. I bet against him.

"Three." The crowd groaned at the losing Come Out roll. The shooter glared at me, as if my bet had caused his downfall. He lifted a drink off the tray of a passing hostess, not even ogling the scant outfit over her tight butt as she walked away. He stalked off, but I was elated; I had enough to pay off Nicky and go back home. Not that I'd ever leave Vegas. Gambling was legal. Prohibition was over. Vegas was the new Wild West, with few laws and fewer lawmen.

I rolled eleven on the Come Out. Nicky came down from his office. No surprise. I was on a streak. The house was losing. I rolled again

"Six. Point."

All my chips were on Pass. Nicky closed the table to everyone but me. I could feel the crowd suck in its breath.

"Double or nothing, Nebraska?" he asked through tight lips.

I nodded, too stupid with greed and revenge to stop myself. I wouldn't lose. I just knew it.

The stickman slid the dice over. I rolled.

"Seven." The stickman scooped the losing combo back.

The neon sign above the club shone through the backseat window in my final ride to the desert. I'll never leave Vegas.

Blind Optimism

Written by Joshua Zepnick

"There are few people whom I really love, and still fewer of whom I think well. The more I see of the world, the more am I dissatisfied with it; and everyday confirms my belief of the inconsistency of all human characters, and of the little dependence that can be placed on the appearance of either merit or sense." - Jane Austen

Amber and Zoe couldn't have been more different. I suppose, if they had really tried, they could have figured out a way to be more opposite; but how to accomplish that is uncertain to me, and probably will be to the reader as well. They were certainly very different. Not only were their names on opposite ends of the alphabetic spectrum, but their personalities and personal lives were polar opposites.

Amber was pure energy. Her thin figure, bright blonde hair, and vivacious smile were contagious, to use an overused word in such circumstances. In high school, she had been the captain of anything and everything with just about nothing left out. At 5 foot 5 inches, she was just the right height. At 122 pounds, she was just the right weight. And with Mr. Right for her significant other, Amber Rayes was just that - a ray of sunshine. And wherever she went, her quippy little one-liners went with her; "Go for the Gold!", "Keep your chin up!", "Wipe that frown off your face; put a smile in its place!", and, her personal favorite, "Don't be sad. Get glad!"

This, as I said, was Amber's personal favorite cliché, but it was Zoe's least favorite. Zoe Wright was a big girl. Her dull, dark brown hair was a mess of curls and tangles. At 5 feet 11 inches and about 220 pounds, she was not predestined for popularity. She was not morbidly obese, but her outlook on life was morbid indeed. She had no real friends and spent most of her time in her bedroom. Zoe had piles of books which she readily consumed and a mattress which she slept on for exactly eight hours every night. She never had a boyfriend and dressed primarily in black clothing to express her deep depression. She tried pills, but they didn't help much. She cut her arms and legs until they looked like one of those maps in an atlas with lines drawn between cities, showing the distance and time of travel. For Zoe, the distance was far between her and the rest of the world, and she was always travelling somewhere in her mind. She kept her travels to herself, as a silent sort of vacation. She was a very quiet girl. According to her high school history teacher, Zoe had a "12-words-a-day quota".

Amber and Zoe both went to Cheyenne Mountain High School. Both graduated in 1992. Amber had a perfect 4.0 grade point average; Zoe carried - or more like dragged - a 2.43. Their mothers were close friends and had also graduated together in the class of 1967. Mrs. Rayes had suggested that the girls get an apartment together for the summer before school. Zoe's mother thought this was a great idea and might help her daughter get out of her permanent residency in the slough of despond. Amber was going to Harvard on a full-ride scholarship. Zoe was going to Pikes Peak Community College, where an aardvark was the mascot.

So they moved in together. Amber immediately took charge. "I want this room! What a view! Zoe, you can have that room and I'm going to go unpack. Let's order takeout and take turns doing dishes and cleaning the bathroom and buying toilet paper and I want to have Steven over at least three times a week and we can have

pizzaforbreakfastandTacoBellforlunchandRamennoodlesatnightlotsofnoodlesthechickenkindand wecanhangoutandhaveagreattimealrightlet'sgetunpacking!" Zoe nodded and made her way to her room. She never said much. Amber was the only one who called Steve Smith "Steven". Or

"Steven Avery Smith" when she was upset with him. But that wasn't too often. They had a near perfect relationship. Or so it appeared.

The girls did have something in common (besides high school and the apartment) - they worked at the same place. Papa Pete's Pizza Plant had been notorious (is that the right word?) for hiring high school and college students for over four decades. Every day, at 5:40 sharp, the two girls went in for their 6 to 2:30 shift, Monday to Friday. They rode together in Amber's car - her '92 Camaro that her dad had bought her as a graduation present. Zoe's rusty Plymouth Reliant sat in the far corner of the apartment parking lot, looking like it was halfway between a mechanic's shop and an auto graveyard. Every morning, the girls were greeted by the image of the fictitious Papa Pete painted on the front of the old factory.

"Chin up, Zoe!" Amber would remind her. "I don't know why you always look like somebody stole your spinach."

That quote made no sense to Zoe. Why spinach? Why not something better, like Steak-ums, or steamed crab, or Swedish

Fish? But she held it in, just like her dad. That was the main reason why her mom had left her dad when Zoe was just fifteen. "That man isn't worth the laundry I fold for him," her mother would say. Zoe didn't say anything. She rarely did. She went home after work, went to her room, and sat there for hours. Sometimes she cried, all alone on her mattress, under her well-placed Genesis poster, with Phil Collins' balding noggin keeping silent company. One thing about Zoe - she was neat. Very organized. Books, records, and clothing in tidy little piles. Well-kept and clutter-free. That was Zoe.

Amber was not as clean, and both Zoe and Steve began to notice it. "Why do you have such a mess in here?" asked Steve one day as he poked his head into Amber's room and was greeted with piles of clothes, candy wrappers, magazines, blankets, and other assorted and
sundry goods.

"Steven Avery Smith, you get out of my room!" snapped Amber, who was washing dishes at the kitchen sink.

"Don't bite my head off!" Steve replied. Then he turned to Zoe, and half-whispered in an aside, "She treats me like I'm a killer or something". Zoe half nodded. "You don't say much, do you?" Steve remarked. Zoe just blushed.

"Steven, leave my friend alone!" retorted Amber. Zoe walked away from the scene and listened to the ensuing argument from the safety of her room. After a few minutes, it was over. They never did argue much, or for long. They looked like the near-perfect couple, from the outside.

"Wipe that frown off your face; put a smile in its place!" Amber started one day; then stopped, mouth agape. Zoe had forgotten to wear a long-sleeve shirt. "Zoe, what did you do to your arms?" Amber inquired with an air of concern which couldn't help but mixing with an air of condescension.

This was one of those rare times when Zoe spoke. "Nothing, just an accident at work," she replied. Six words. Half of her quota for the day.

"Uh-huh," Amber retorted. "I told you before - don't get sad; get glad!" When it came to Amber and Zoe, there was always some misunderstanding, always some kind of mistake.

Work kept on the same through June and July. Early August, however, Papa Pete recruited some new faces. One of these was Justin, who seemed to stand out from the rest. He was a great worker, helpful to others, and unusually polite. One day, he came and sat next to Zoe, who was (as usual) alone. "I see you sitting here every day by yourself," he started. "Are you doing all right?"

"Yeah, I guess," she replied, not making eye contact.

"How long have you been here?"

"Two-two… and a half…months," she shyly stammered.

"I like it here. This is a good job," Justin started. Apparently he was oblivious to the horrid stench of the rotting bad crust container, and the stains all over the break room floor, and the antiquated everything around the plant, and the low pay without benefits. "Will you be my friend?" he asked. The question caught Zoe by surprise. Something within her lit.

"Sure, but I don't have any friends. You seem different. Why are you different?" She surpassed her daily quota in an avalanche of words.

Justin smiled, then explained, "I am a Christian. Jesus changed my life. Do you have a Bible?" Zoe didn't. "Here, take this one."

Zoe looked for a minute at the black leather cover, with the words "Holy Bible: King James Version" on the front. "Thank you," she said as she put the book into her lunch box and headed back into the plant.

During the rest of the day at work, Zoe's mind was busy. It was always busy, but it was especially busy for the remainder of the workday. So much was on her mind. Life. School coming up. Finally someone had reached out to her. And the Bible? Why had no one offered her one before? She had always had a vague belief in God, but this was like some kind of invisible touch by Him into her world. Then her thoughts returned home. "Funny," she thought. "I haven't seen Steve for at least a week. It's never been more than three days before... And come to think of it, Amber hasn't been much the same either. She's been somewhat quieter and to herself."

The next morning, Zoe woke up at the usual time of 5:15am. and got ready to go. She even looked for a few minutes at the Bible so graciously gifted her the previous day. But now it was time to go to work. Ah, yes! Today was August 19 - Amber's golden birthday! But where was Amber? It was 5:40. Zoe knocked on Amber's door. It was the first time she had done this, as usually it was Amber wanting to get into Zoe's room to talk to her. "Amber, Amber! Happy birthday!" No reply at all. A few minutes later, she knocked again. Nothing. "Amber, this isn't funny! It's time to go." A couple long minutes of silence followed. It was now 5:46. Time seemed to stand still. "Amber we're going to be late for work!" Zoe complained. Not yet 6am, and Zoe was seven words over her quota. 5:48, and she could no longer wait.

Zoe opened the door slowly and saw her friend lying face down on the bed. She grunted and mumbled under her breath, "Lazy..." Her eyes caught a piece of paper lying on the side of the bed. Zoe picked it up and started to read it. "Amber," it began. Zoe stopped. It was obviously in Steve's writing, but he normally began his notes with something flowery like "Dear Amber." or "Dearest Amber," or "Sweet Princess," or "To My Little Honey Bunches of Oats," or something along those lines. Zoe knew because she had seen love letters lying around on the kitchen table. Just plain "Amber" was too terse. Something was wrong. Zoe didn't really want to be nosy, but her friend was sound asleep. She continued reading. "Amber: I can't go on with you anymore. I know you are a fake who's been cheating on me. I know about your pill habit. The talks we have had in the last week aren't getting anywhere. Why don't you do us all a favor and take all of your pills. I hate you. Steven."

Zoe recoiled in horror. As she looked up, her eyes caught the sight of empty pill bottles - clear and orangish - scattered on her nightstand. Zoe felt sick to her stomach. This couldn't really be happening. Her fingers trembled as her hands moved toward Amber. Gingerly, yet frantically, she felt the pulse of her optimistically-oriented friend. Nothing. "AMBER!" Zoe screamed. Above the bed, a clean poster of a smiling young man had these words on it: "Don't get sad. Get glad!"

An Uncommonly Sunny Day

Written by Ramona Scarborough

The day Fenton Ferguson's universe turned upside down began like any other. He rousted himself out of bed and then remade it to hotel standards. Neatly, he folded his striped pajamas. He scrubbed vigorously in the shower, shaved, and combed what was left of his hair.

His usual breakfast, an egg boiled for three minutes and twenty seconds, and bread toasted to a perfect tan, were washed down with a strong cup of coffee. He gulped down the blue, green, and white pills Dr. Guggenheim had prescribed. The dishes rinsed off and put in the dishwasher in an orderly fashion, he dressed in his work uniform of dark pants, black dress shoes, and white shirt. Fenton knotted his tie carefully, making sure it was centered exactly between the points of his collar.

In his apartment's parking garage, he slid into the front seat of his Toyota Corolla and headed for the exit.

"Boy, it's going to be another hot one," he thought, as he guided his car into the lane of traffic. At the first red light, he turned on the radio to get a weather report. Idly, he glanced up through the windshield. He blinked. He leaned forward, his hands gripping the steering wheel tighter.

A horn blared. An orange-haired woman leaned out her car window behind him and hollered at him. "There's only one shade of green, bub!"

Fenton eased his car into first gear and moved forward, but kept his eyes glued on the sky. *Crash*! His Toyota's bumper smashed into the back of a delivery truck. In a domino effect, the angry lady's SUV rammed into him, crumpling the Toyota's trunk like it was corrugated cardboard.

The delivery truck driver pulled to the curb and jumped out. Fenton wanted to follow suit, but the rest of the block was parked full. Stiffly, he climbed out of his car.

"Hey, why don't you watch where you're going?" The hulking driver shouted. The woman barreled out of her car shaking her fist.

"You idiot, you can't be stargazing while driving. You should have your license revoked. It's your fault I ran into you."

Fenton swallowed. "I hope you're not hurt."

"Well, that remains to be seen," she said. "I could have whiplash."

"Look," he said, pointing upward. "That's why I had my eyes on the sky. I'll bet you didn't even notice."

"Notice what?" she said, tilting her head back and shading her eyes. The truck driver got out of his vehicle and hurried over.

"Don't you see? There's ... TWO suns, not one, TWO."

"Huh?" the trunk driver said, frowning as he gazed at the familiar sky.

The woman hit her palm on her forehead. "Oh, great, I've run into a certified crackpot. Are you seeing double because you went out on a bender last night?" She stabbed her finger heavenward. "There's one sun and one sun only, you bozo."

By this time, with the lane blocked, horns were honking and drivers were shouting. Fenton hollered over the noise. "You honestly can't see them?"

The woman jammed her fists on her ample waist. "No, I can't, but I can definitely see the damage to my new Suburban."

Insurance information exchanged, Fenton and his injured car limped to a nearby parking garage. He punched in his work number.

"Hi Gail. Is Mr. Bergren available?"

While he listened to hold music, a jangling version of "It's a Small World," he ducked his head to see outside. The two suns stubbornly hovered above the horizon.

"Ferguson," his boss growled in his ear, startling Fenton. "You know our company doesn't tolerate employees coming in late."

"Mr. Bergren, I had an accident on the way to work. I won't be able to come in. I need to call my insurance company and have my car towed. I'm sure they'll give me a loaner and I can be in tomorrow."

"All right, but we don't want to get behind on the Sherman account."

After pressing end, Fenton slumped over the steering wheel and closed his eyes. Was he going crazy? He'd been in therapy for years, but mainly for an obsessive-compulsive disorder and his inability to make connections with people. Maybe he'd tipped over into another dimension of being unbalanced.

Instead of calling his insurance agent, he slowly got out of his car, rubbed his sore neck, and walked out onto the sidewalk. The two suns blazed down. He loosened his tie, took out his pocket handkerchief and wiped his broad forehead.

Cars whizzed by and people walked past, some talking on their cell phones, some looking straight ahead, obviously not one of them aware of the phenomenon in the sky above them.

Suddenly, all Fenton wanted to do was go home. Only seven blocks from his apartment, he decided to walk; maybe it would clear his head. He kept scanning the sky every few steps, but the twin suns remained steadfast.

For the second time that fateful day, his inattentiveness caused an accident. He bowled right into a woman.

"So sorry," he said. Looking at the person he'd ran into, he saw she was crying. "Oh, did I hurt you?"

She looked at the ground and shook her head. "No, I'm alright. I mean, I'm not alright, but it's not because of you."

"Can I do anything to help?" Fenton asked.

She shook her head again. "No, it's just that no one will believe me. I think maybe I'm losing my mind."

"Really? Try me."

She pushed her glasses down to the tip of her nose. "Look up at the sky. Tell me what you see."

"Well, maybe you'll think I'm crazy. There's two suns up there, not one, but two."

The woman grabbed his shoulders and jumped up and down. "Yes, yes, two suns! I went outside this morning to let my cat out and there they were. How come nobody else spots this amazing occurrence?"

"I have no idea. By the way, I'm Fenton Ferguson."

The woman let go of him, her face flushing with embarrassment. "Sorry, I'm just so relieved to know I'm not the only person who saw it. I'm Ayla Jones. Do you think it could be aliens trying to communicate with us?"

"Hm-m, I hadn't thought of that. But why us? Maybe we have something in common that made them pick us? Say, do you have to be somewhere, like work or something? Maybe we could go have coffee and talk about this."

"No, I work from home, I make craft items and sell them on Etsy. I mean, yes, I'd like to go. There's a coffee shop on Sixth Street."

"Oh, yeah, Brews for You."

They began walking, sneaking glimpses at over-occupied space above their heads. Ayla laughed nervously. "Unfortunately, the second one is still there."

Fenton laughed along with her.

"So, what do you do?" Ayla asked.

"I'm a software engineer for Bergren and Associates, but I had a car accident this morning staring at our unparalleled event. I'm taking the day off to contact my insurance company and get the car towed."

Ayla shook her head and her dark chin length hair swished around her heart shaped face. "Oh, did you get hurt?"

"Well, my neck's kind of sore."

"You should have it checked."

When they settled in a booth at the coffee shop, Fenton already knew what he wanted, so while Ayla was intent on the menu, he had a chance to look at her closely.

Her black bangs brushed the top of her eyebrows. Her fingernails were short and unpolished. Her turquoise glasses balanced on the bridge of a sharp nose. Everything else about her was round, her cheeks, her breasts, and her hips, an altogether pleasing picture.

When she looked up, he fixed his eyes on the tables in the center of the room. "What are you having?" she said, smiling.

"An Americano, I like strong coffee."

"Me too."

When the coffee and pastries came, she turned the plate

around, rearranged the cup on the saucer and cut the maple bar into exact bite-sized pieces. Ayla looked up as she stirred cream into her coffee. "Don't you think this is kind of exciting, Fenton? I mean, it's a real mystery. Do you have any ideas?"

"I'll Google two suns on my phone and see what I come up with."

He frowned as he looked at the screen. "Well, it appears "Two Suns" is a song by Pink Floyd, not much help. I think that, because so far we're the only ones observing this rarity, we must have some connection."

A whole hour passed comparing similarities. There were many.

"Well, I'd best get calling about my car," he said, finally. He cleared his throat. "Uh, do you think you'd consider going on a date with me?"

"Uh … well." She fidgeted with a Celtic ring on her right hand. "I think I ought to tell you, I've got a lot of… of hang-ups. I go for therapy on Wednesday mornings with Dr. Guggenheim."

"You're kidding. I see him on Wednesday evenings."

Ayla sat silent for a few moments. "Wait a minute," she said, sitting up straight. "Did he give you that new white pill?"

"Yes, he said this experimental drug might help me relax."

"He gave me one too." She gestured toward the ceiling. "Do you think this has anything to do with… you know?"

"I think we need to call him."

Ayla began to giggle. "I wonder if it has any other side effects."

That night, Fenton and Ayla sat on a park bench holding hands as they watched the two moons rising.

Save the Date

Written by Barbara Herrera

It was the date of a lifetime. Everything was perfect, from dinner at the restaurant to a walk on the moonlit beach. By now, it was standard operating procedure — every date with Babe had been perfect. All one hundred and eighty-four of them. Not that I was keeping track, of course.

It was also no surprise when Babe got down on one knee and pulled out the most beautiful ring. I had never been one to go along with silly traditions just for the sake of tradition, but I must admit that I was eager to become *Mrs. Babe*. I had been dreaming of the question for so long that I nearly forgot to wait until I was asked! The answer was a resounding yes.

I was floating on air the whole way home; I just couldn't wait to visit Sparky and tell her the good news. She had been my best friend for as long as I could remember, although I wasn't always sure why; she never failed to get me involved in situations I'd rather avoid. Still, she had been my best friend since before my parents died — she had to be my first announcement.

Sparky wasted no time planning my bachelorette party. I did have my own stipulations, though.

"No strippers."

"Got it. No cheap strippers."

"*No,* Sparky. I'm serious. Absolutely. No. Strippers."

Sparky sighed, but relented. "Fine. No strippers. But you know this hurts me."

I laughed. "I'm sure it does. I promise, we can have strippers at *your* bachelorette."

Sparky raised an eyebrow in response. "We both know I'm *never* getting married. There isn't a man alive who can handle *all this.*" She emphatically motioned at her entire body. I had to admit, she was a lot to handle sometimes.

"And no all-nighters," I added after some pause. Sparky just stared blankly at me. "I have to be at work in the morning."

"You don't even know what day it's going to be."

"I get up *every day*, Sparks."

"I mean… if you *want* to go to sleep at your party, I guess I'll try not to take it too personally." I sighed and rolled my eyes, but she continued. "It's not like you have time to ask for the next day off or something." She added in the puppy dog eyes — my absolute weakness! — and I caved.

No matter how many times I asked, Sparky refused to tell me what her party plans were. I could basically count on it being something wild, but it drove me insane not knowing. With how adamantly she refused to give me any hints, I was almost certain there would be strippers and debauchery involved, too. It would be unrealistic to expect anything different from her.

I spent the next few months sorting out the details of the wedding itself, and that helped to keep my mind off the bachelorette party. I was still nervous because I had no idea what to expect, but I trusted Sparky implicitly. Even if her choices were sometimes despicable, they always came from a good place. If I pushed myself to have more fun without her, she wouldn't feel the need to push me as much as she did.

As expected, Sparky gave me less than 24 hours notice before picking me up for my bachelorette party, but she assured me she had already worked it out with my boss. Babe confirmed. I breathed a sigh of relief; at least Sparky had help with this plan. Maybe it wouldn't be so bad after all. She did make me put on a blindfold as I climbed into her messy car. I took a deep breath and tried to remain calm. My heart was beating out of my throat.

I recognized the first stop before I even removed the blindfold. It was the bar that we had our first legal drinks at. Truth be told, it wasn't the first bar we ever drank in, but something about ditching the fake IDs had made it feel so much more special. They still had the same Friday night band that they had when we were in college, and it still smelled like the same cheap vodka and menthol cigarettes. This bar was where I'd met Babe, too. I smiled. She *had* put some thought into this after all.

It only took a few minutes for us to get a table, in part because Sparky wouldn't stop yelling, "MacGuffin is getting married y'all!" It was embarrassing, to say the least, but it got us the best table in the house. Some of the regulars here had practically watched us grow up, so many sent their congratulations in the form of the frilliest, girliest drinks on the menu. It wasn't long before we had more than we could drink responsibly. Sparky happily swigged any I passed up, and even sent a few leftovers to some younger guys who had clearly already had enough. Sparky got drunk much quicker than I did, in part because she was double-fisting and in part because she was only five feet tall. I walked outside and hoped that she would be out soon after. It seemed like at least a half hour passed before she emerged on the arm of one of the younger guys, who now stood before me shirtless. His shirt, I soon noticed, was wrapped tightly around Sparky's right hand.

"Great, Sparks. A bar fight? Really?"

Sparky gave a half-hearted smirk. "Not a bar fight. Just a misunderstanding in the lady's room." She was clearly too drunk for me to hold this over her for long, but I made a stern face to threaten that I might. "I'm sorry, Guffs. I tried to be good, really I did."

Muscles spoke up to defend her. "It's my fault, really. I followed her in there and... Didn't realize my girlfriend was following me."

"Jesus, Sparky!" I exclaimed. "He has a girlfriend, too?!"

That's when Sparky's drunken smile crept wider. "Well, not *anymore*." I crossed my arms. "What's next?"

Muscles spoke up again. "My bros and I were on our way to a house party. You ladies are welcome to tag along." I couldn't help but laugh. Muscle bros at a house party were *not* my idea of a fun time, but Sparky insisted.

"Come *on*, MacGuffin. It's your last night as a single lady! Aren't you ready to celebrate?" I sighed. The wedding was still over a month away, but clearly she'd already made up her (very drunk) mind. So much for my night!

We made the responsible choice to walk the few blocks to the party; I even took Sparky's keys so I felt safer. Muscles clicked the lock on his car as we passed by: a bright orange Charger with custom vanity plates. "CARMUH" — exactly the type of lame joke you'd expect from someone who looked like he did.

The party itself wasn't as bad as I pictured. The music was decent, and a few random college girls even asked me about my ring. It still wasn't an ideal Friday evening, but it was better than being kicked out of the bar. I didn't have much time to enjoy it, though; not even an hour after our arrival, Sparky grabbed me by the arm and ran out of the house. I was so confused, but pleased that Muscles didn't follow us back out to the street.

As the house faded into the background, I asked Sparky what that was all about. Without a word, she pulled a wad of cash and little baggies out of her pocket. My jaw hit the pavement. Sparky didn't sell drugs... She must have lifted them off someone at the party.

"I really don't know what to say about you. You said you had these fun plans made for me, but are you just dragging me along for some mischief or what?!" I shouted. Sparky's smile slowly faded into a scowl and she shoved the money back in her pocket.

"You used to be so much fun, Guff. Like, *the best*. What happened?"

"I'm still fun," I objected.

"Yeah, I guess, but you used to be *fun* fun. Now you're just... Adult fun." She looked genuinely disappointed by this. I didn't know what she expected out of this conversation. She was too drunk to be reasonable. I didn't dignify it with a response. After a few minutes of walking, Sparky let out a squeal. "This is it! This is our third stop!" As if to prove to me that this had been the plan all along, she shoved up her sleeve to show me an address written in marker on her arm. *534 Wicker Street*. The building in front of us read *534 Wicker Street*, too. Certainly the night couldn't get much worse than it already was.

When we entered the small, crowded foyer, an old woman with a weathered face met us. She extended her hands and greeted us both by name. Sparky and I exchanged an awkward glance as she placed a hand on each of our shoulders and hummed to herself. After a moment, she went through the door in the back of the room and came back out holding a large deck of cards. We sat spread around the table in the center of the room and Sparky pulled out a handful of cash from the wad in her pocket, but the old woman shook her head.

"That money is no good here."

Sparky stammered. "The money is good, I promise." The old woman resisted still. I let out a sigh and pulled out some cash from my own pocket. Babe had sent me with a bit just in case Sparky had forgotten her wallet at home. This was just as good a situation as any to use it.

The old woman grabbed the money and began flipping cards. She seemed to read from a script as she spoke to us. *"You"* — she sneered at Sparky — "have upset the entire universe. And *you*" — she now tipped her head toward me — "will lose a very dear family member soon." No sooner had the words left her mouth than she slumped over in her chair. I felt cheated. The only part of my bachelorette party that was actually about me, and it was cut short by an apparent nap attack.

I stormed out of the shop and headed back toward the bar. I needed to head home; not that I necessarily believed the old woman's words, but if she *was* telling my future, I had to be sure that Babe was OK. I didn't have any other family. It was just me, Babe, and Sparky.

A few minutes later, Sparky came running up behind me, her pockets overflowing with booty she'd looted from the psychic shop. She laughed as she held up the crystal spears, the heavy glass beads, and even a small brass bowl.

"As if you hadn't done enough," I cried. "You've *ruined* my bachelorette party. You always do this." I hadn't meant for it to come across so harsh; sure, she always did things like this, but I should have grown to expect it by now.

Before she had time to answer, or put the pilfered goods back in her pockets, a car came speeding around the corner and ran her down. The crystals and beads and cash and cocaine flew all over the street. I was in shock. The brightly-colored flash of metal hadn't even bothered to slow down when they hit her. Their license plate had flown off in the crash, so I walked over to pick it up, certain that the police would ask for it when I made the call. I wiped off Sparky's blood.

CARMUH.

Love and Loss

Written by Ramah Juta

His eyes clouded with tears. Fortunately, they did not run down his cheeks. The nurse had walked away to give him a private moment. He hugged Helena tightly. She was blissfully unaware that this place would be her future home. He felt as if a part of his life was being detached from him.

David returned to an empty home. A pall of darkness enveloped him. He felt lonely and depressed. He was wracked with guilt, but there was no alternative. Age and health issues had eventually caught up with him.

There was a knock on the door and his daughter Jodi walked in. She hugged him and he sobbed like a baby. She reassured him and said, 'Dad, you did your level best. The situation was not in your hands any more. Come and sit at the table. I will warm the chicken and vegetables." She took out two plates, in the hope that he would eat if he had company. He nibbled at the food.

Later he changed into his pyjamas. After giving him a glass of warm milk Jodi left. She promised to return the next day. It had been a difficult and traumatic day for him. He lay in bed with eyes closed but sleep escaped him. The movie of his life played before him. He had been the principal of a primary school, and happily married to childhood sweetheart Rachael. They were soon blessed with a daughter and she was called Jodi. His parents, who lived round the corner, adored her, as she was their only grandchild.

School holidays were a time to travel within Australia. Their old but reliable car took them to the different states. Rachael was great at organizing the holidays and booked hotels or caravan parks.

When Jodi was ten years old, her mum felt a lump in her breast. Surgery, radiotherapy and chemotherapy followed. However the creepy, crawly cancer sent its tentacles to her liver and lungs. She was a spiritual person and remained strong and positive. In spite of this, Rachael succumbed to the cancer. David was devastated but life had to carry on. He was young and resilient.

Work was a panacea. As a single parent, life was busy. At night he tucked Jodi into bed and read her a story. With the support of his parents, he managed to live a balanced life. Rachael's sisters also assisted when needed. Jodi enjoyed being with her cousins and stayed with them occasionally. The years galloped away. Jodi grew up to be a well-adjusted lady and qualified as a teacher. She developed wings and David retired.

He went for a morning run, played golf, and joined a yoga class. Taking day trips with other seniors was enjoyable. Thus he was able to go to Palm Beach, Blue Mountains, and other places. The library remained his favourite place, as he was a voracious reader.

Joining Rotary opened new paths for him and changed his world. He met Helena, a very pretty woman. He was attracted to her and his heart skipped a beat. She was delightful company and he took hesitant steps in wooing her. Between work as a qualified nurse and caring for her fragile old mum, life was busy. When mum departed this world, there was time for herself. Thus she joined Rotary, a writing group, and did community gardening.

She was Greek and fifteen years younger than him. David was physically and mentally young. He still had a good crop of grey curly hair. He met Helena's numerous uncles and aunts who delighted in feeding him. Jodi was overjoyed for her dad. She said, "Live your life to the fullest. You have been a single dad for long enough. Also, your parents have passed away. I am going out with James and will introduce him to you soon."

With this reassurance, David proposed to Helena. She accepted and they married at a simple civil ceremony. A Greek feast followed. David booked an Eastern Mediterranean cruise. He chose this particular cruise because it covered Mykonos, Santorini, and Athens, in addition to the other destinations. It was the very first overseas trip for both!

They returned refreshed and settled down to normal life. Helena loved the garden. The fresh produce arrived as a scrumptious meal. Dinner was light. Usually David made soup or sandwiches while Helena went for an evening walk. It was her time of peace, relaxation, and rumination. She liked daylight savings and dusk invited the sound of cicadas.

Helena was an organized and meticulous person. She rearranged a few things in the kitchen. Jodi was happy that Rachael's photographs still took pride of place in the lounge and dining room. She did not want the memory of her mum erased. David and Helena kept busy with Rotary activities. They gave each other space to follow their own activities. David met his friends while she went to her writing group or listened to Greek music.

Cruising was their favourite way of seeing the world. They visited the Baltic States, Alaska, and Antarctica. Taking part in onboard activities added to their pleasure. They danced and watched shows together. David read books while Helena went to the gym and Zumba. Life was a breeze and David tasted happiness again. It was always great to return home where basic food supplies awaited them, as Jodi had their house keys.

The years flew by. David still looked good and was active in spite of having a heart problem. Slowly but steadily, Helena's mood became unpredictable. David noticed subtle changes, which he overlooked. She was taking longer to do simple tasks and made a mess when cooking. House keys went missing and finally appeared in the cutlery drawer! On one occasion, Helena went for her usual walk and could not find her way home. Fortunately, a kindly neighbour guided her home. Washed clothes landed up in the wrong drawers. She was frustrated when she could not find her undies. He found them among the sheets!

Deeply concerned, David took her to the doctor who took a detailed history. He did a Mini Mental test and ordered blood tests and an MRI and CT. Doctor thought that Helena had mild cognitive impairment. They returned home and Helena complained, "Why did the doctor ask me silly questions like the date of the month and day of the week? I am not working so I don't care." She was upset that she had to go for blood tests and further investigations.

David pacified her saying, "You remember I had to have investigations when I had a heart problem."

What a relief when Helena responded, "I remember investigations and blood tests were done when I worked as a nurse. Mum also had regular blood tests." This was a sign that her long term memory was good.

On the follow up visit Helena was referred to a geriatrician who felt that Helena had early stage Alzheimer's disease. He said, "Sometimes sporadic cases occur at an early age. I will start her on Aricept. Hopefully it helps her."

After their evening walk, Helena listened to music. David did his research on the computer. He learnt that Alzheimer's did not discriminate. Black, white, brown, rich and poor, premiers and presidents came within its grasp. He was familiar with the grey and white matter of the brain. He read about amyloid plaques and neurofibrillary tangles, which impair signals passing through brain cells. He hoped that the Aricept would slow or stop the dementing process.

He set up a routine. She set the table for breakfast. He allowed her to make the scrambled eggs while he toasted the bread. Later they sat and watched the morning news. Helena had her shower while he read the newspaper.

When in the garden, she was happy and told him the name of all the flowers. While watering the plants, she sprayed him and had a giggle. In the afternoon they played cards and solved puzzles. He encouraged her to join him in simple exercise. Music helped and she got him up to dance.

David made sure that she took her daily dose of Aricept. She started on 5mg and was later increased to 10mg. The whole pattern of life changed. Basically, he took charge of the home situation. When clothes were washed, he both hung them on the line and folded them. He tried to supervise the meal preparation but she preferred to be boss in the kitchen. The main problem was that she often forgot to switch off the stove.

There was a slow and steady deterioration. The situation became very stressful for David. He realized that it was easier to care for a growing child than an adult who was going downhill. It was pure irony that the older David was caring for the younger Helena. Life is full of uncertainties! Eventually he opted for adult day care twice a week. Transport, meals, supervised music and exercise were provided. It gave David a chance to come out of the house, do shopping and visit the library, his place of peace.

Helena was always happy to return home from daycare. Without fail, she hugged David. Also she did not complain about going to daycare. A lady came in for help with showering and personal care. She was Greek and Helena was cooperative.

With this regime, time glided by. Nobody is immune to the ageing process. Soon David developed a slight tremor. The doctor called it an "essential tremor." It was mild but it did affect his life. The knee joints squeaked and stiffened. Fortunately the house was single level and the pain was relieved with simple analgesics. Jodi visited whenever she could. Helena had forgotten who she was and accused her of being the "other woman."

David finally gave up when his wife could not manage her bodily functions. She did not even know who he was. Jodi did the search for "dementia specific" homes. She discussed everything with dad and made the necessary arrangements. He found the whole process traumatic. She arranged a cab so he could personally take her to the nursing home.

It had been an overwhelming day. He had loved and he had lost. He fell into a deep sleep, never to wake up again.

Black Death

Written by L'oreal Nicole Lee

Hi, my name is Dr. John Smith; I am from London, England. I am now 75 years old and have seen all I need to see. I am going to tell you all a little bit about the things that I have seen. It all started back in 1563 in London; I had just finished working on a case about an unknown disease. I was just about to leave my office, when there was a knock on my door; it was my dear friend Dr. Lee. As I opened the door, I saw a look of terror on his face. He was a pale color, his skin had black lumps and red spots with little rings around them everywhere.

"Come, come in," I said to him. "What's wrong, Dr. Lee?"

He looked at me like a scared child wanting to be rescued from the big bad monster and said, "I…I don't know. I was hoping you could tell me Dr. Smith." Then for a few moments he hung his head down, then he looked at me again, "There are many others like me." As those words flowed out his mouth, my mind and heart began to race rapidly as though they were two racehorses trying to be the first to the finish line. Thoughts of what it could be that was making my friend and others sick like these was still racing rapidly through my mind. Then it hit me like a freight train: a plague had hit London like a tsunami. While I was so wrapped up in my thoughts, I did not realize that Dr. Lee had stopped breathing. I shook him frantically, but it was no use; he was dead.

I quickly called the coroner to come and remove his body. When he arrived and saw Dr. Lee, he looked as if he had never seen a dead corpse before. "D-D-D-D-Dr. Smith, what is that on his skin?" he said with a horrifying look on his face.

"I'm not sure exactly, I need you to examine him and find out what we are dealing with, and quickly. I'm afraid that this is only the beginning, there are many more like him and your office will soon be flooded with their bodies."

As the horrifying look turned to terror he said, "I...I...I'll get right on it, Dr. Smith." He then placed my dear old friend in a body bag.

"Farewell, dear friend. Farewell." I said as he took him away.

I immediately departed my office after the coroner left to go see Queen Mary and request that she grant me permission and royal researchers to help me research and found out what is happening to her people. When I entered the queen's palace, she was weeping uncontrollably. Then she cried out, "My son, my beautiful son." I looked to my right and saw him lying still. I quickly walked over to observe him. He looked just like Dr. Lee had when he came to my office earlier that morning.

I walked back over to the queen and knelt down before, " My Queen, I ask your permission to gather a group of your royal researchers to help me find out what is happening to your son and people?" She granted me my request and begged me to hurry.

I went to see the coroner. He said that he could not figure out what it was that was causing this sickness and what it did to the body inside and out was nothing like anything he had ever seen before. I thanked him for his help and left. When I got back to my office, I immediately went to work. About 300 people died that day. It was the most horrifying thing London had ever seen. I worked night and day, trying and trying to figure out how I could cure this outbreak but had no success. About 19,700 more died day after day for three years straight.

In 1567, I left London after the plague to continue my research and maybe have more success in helping others survive this "Black Death" that had invaded Europe. My destination was Sarajevo. While en route, I found out that there was a typhoid fever epidemic going on. When I arrived, they took me straight to the most intense case. When I walked into the patient's room, his body was covered by red rashes, his nose was bloody, his temperature was a 104, and he was constipated. Back in London I had worked on many vaccines and some antibiotics to cure my people, none had worked, and I was not sure they would work now, but I had to try.

I observed and treated this patient for many weeks. During my observation I discovered that the infectious disease was transmitted to them from the livestock that they were eating. I had given him many different vaccines but none were successful. I had not tried the antibiotics; they were my last hope. I gave them to him in small doses because I was unsure of how his body would respond to them.

After a few days of the treatment, I began to see an improvement in his health. I gradually gave him stronger doses and, in about three weeks, he was cured. I treated and cured many others, but still the disease had claimed 100,000 lives. I realize that was about 80,000 more lives than in London that had fallen victim to this disease. I was gracious that I was able to help many survive.

It was a year before I had heard about another plague. Then in 1569, I heard that the inhabitants of Lisbon were dying from something called the carbuncular fever epidemic. So once again, I started tracking down the disease that was about to claim some many lives. Little did I know that it had already claimed 50% of the lives it would take. That was about 20,000 lives it had taken before I reached Lisbon.

When I arrived, families were weeping, people were laid out in the streets, and livestock looked like it had not been fed in weeks. I could not figure out how to ease the pain these inhabitants were feeling. It was depressing for me because once again I was in a position where I could not even help just one, just like in London. For as long as I had been a doctor, I was always able to save at least one life in each case, but this time I could only stand by and watch these inhabitants suffer and suffer until they died.

For three months, I worked nonstop on a vaccine to help ease their pain. I finally found one but by then it was too late. The carbuncular fever epidemic ended a few months later, but not before it claimed a total of 40,000 lives.

It was almost 5 years before I got my next case. It was 1575; I was 41 years of age when an outbreak of a plague hit Sicily. I moved quickly to get there before the outbreak got too big to control. I did not want a recurrence of Lisbon. I reached Sicily in two days and got straight to work. I had already researched the plague and created a vaccine. My assistants and I began giving the vaccine to the major cases first. Then the minor ones. We told the people that they could not travel outside of Sicily until they had received the vaccine. It took about three weeks to give everyone the vaccine. That night I went over the list of residences to make sure that everyone had received the shot. I stumbled across one individual whose name was not crossed off.

The next morning, I went to his cottage to see why he had not come to receive his vaccination. I stood and pounded on the door for about 20 minutes but there was no answer. I walked around the side to look in the window; he had packed up and left. I went into the cottage; it looked like he had left in a hurry. There was food on the table, the radio was on, and there was a tub full of water. I looked around for clues of where he might go, then I came across a letter. It read:

"To whom it may concern,
I have left Sicily and traveled to Rosolini to get away from this plague. I have been in good health all my life and I plan to stay that way.

Farewell,
Leon Alejandro"

As I read the letter my chest began to tighten, my legs became weak, and it became hard to breathe. I was in shock over what I had just read. The words had overtaken me as though it was a plague of its own. Once I had snapped back to reality, I knew I had to move quickly, for another city was in danger of being infected. When I arrived, I informed the authorities about the Sicilian man I was looking for. I started searching around asking others as well if they had seen him. My search lasted for two days, then, about 3:00 am on Tuesday morning, I received a message from a Dr. Adams.

He requested my presence at his hospital. I got dressed and headed to the hospital. When I arrived, I was greeted by a tall and skinny young man. His hair was a copper color and he had the face of a child. "Are you one of Dr. Adam's assistants?" I asked.

"No, no, Dr. Smith. I am Dr. Adams."

"Welcome to Rosolini," he said as he shook my hand. We headed inside of the facility, as we walked, he began telling me about a man that he had there from Sicily. He said the man was covered from head to toe with ulcers and concomitant swelling on the knee. As I listen to Dr. Adams, I prayed that the man had not come in contact with anyone, but I knew that it was impossible not to.

When we entered his room, I began asking the man whom he had come in contact with. He had come in contact with about 30 people. I knew that 20 times as many people were infected now and it was too late to vaccinate the whole city. About 12 noon, we began giving out vaccinations until we ran out. I heard that the population in London had decreased to only 300,000 and, sadly, when I thought about the reason why I began to sob, thinking about how I had helped so many others but I couldn't even save one of my people. I knew I could not go back there.

About 16 years had passed by before my expertise was called upon once again. It was a hard time for me because I had to live on a normal salary. It was chump change compared to what I was making during my travels. I had become a professor at the University of Edinburgh in Scotland when it was founded in 1583. This was seven years after "Black Death" had left five cities in discomfort. It was 1592 and, as I was teaching a class, I received a message that another plague had hit London and it had already claimed 1,000 lives. I had no choice but to go back now. This was God giving me a second chance to help my people.

It took me about two days to gather all my research and

belongings. Saturday morning, I set off for London. I arrived Sunday afternoon and was escorted to London's research facility. When I arrived, I was met by a short, chubby man by the name of Dr. Johnson. He had also been doing research on the plagues. He told me how lucky I was to be able to have a hands-on research experience "Black Death" and he envied me for it. I told him it was nothing lucky about it. Watching as all those people have suffered from these horrifying and painful diseases.

After an hour of comparing notes, we began our new research; by this time, the plague had taken 10,000 lives total. We worked anxiously on a vaccine for two weeks before we created the right one. We went to visit homes to hand out the vaccines. By that time, it had claimed 15,000 lives total, but it was over and I had helped save my people. I stayed a little while longer to help Dr. Johnson finish up his research.

A few days before I was set to head back to Scotland, I read that London theaters had been closed due to some unknown infestation. As a lump formed in my throat I knew that I had been bamboozled by the "Black Death" and that it wasn't finished with London yet. Dr. Johnson and I were called in to help disinfect the theaters. We created a spray to use to wash down the theaters. It took us 6 months to effectively disinfect each theater. In May of 1593, the London theaters were reopened. Soon after, I return to the University of Edinburgh to continue teaching until my services were required again.

The Old Man

Written by Clay Harris

He dug his old fingers into the ground and scraped away the loose dirt with his nails. The soil was dry and the worms were scarce. It had not rained in weeks and the heat baked the ground into fine powdered dust. Behind him, the bayou flowed dark and slow, cutting a narrow path through the thick canopy of grey moss that hung tangled in the branches of the ancient cypress trees. The old man took his pliers from his pocket and stabbed the earth with their dulled point, breaking up the hard ground. He saw the tail of a worm escaping deeper into the dirt. He grabbed the tail between his thin fingers and loosened the dirt around it with the pliers, lifting the worm out whole.

"He should do, Jess," the man said over his shoulder. There was no answer. He grabbed his cane pole and took the rusty hook in his hand. With care, the old man fed one end of the worm onto the hook, moved the worm down, and hooked his middle, then hooked him once more towards his bottom. He let the baited hook drop into the dust and adjusted the orange bobber so the hook would sit just above the bottom of the muddy bayou floor. Satisfied, the old man bent slowly and picked his pole from the dust. "Now we're ready, Jess," he said.

He swung the line out into the dark water. The orange bobber sunk on impact then settled still atop the water. The old man sat his pole on the bank and squatted down to watch the bobber. He ran his dirty fingers through his tangled grey beard and scratched his chin. Sweat ran down his brow and the back of his neck. Thunder rolled in the distance.

He looked towards the sky. "Hear that, Jess? Thunder. Need some rain."

He stared at the bobber, still and motionless in the unmoving black water, as if the heat had convinced even the water that it was too hot to flow. Thunder clapped again, this time louder, and closer.

A turtle poked its head out of the water near the old man's line. The turtle looked around and sank back under.

"You stay away from my worm, you hear?" the old man yelled at the turtle. Just then, the bobber popped up and down, sending little ripples through the still water. "You damn turtle!" The old man lifted his line from the water and checked his bait. The turtle had bitten the worm in half, leaving the rest dangling loose and wet on the rusted hook. "There's still enough left to catch us some dinner, Jess."

He swung the line out and landed it softly in the water. Again, he squatted down and waited. Minutes passed, and there was no action. Thunder cracked. The wind grew fierce and blew the moss sideways in the cypress trees. Rain began to pour down. The rain rippled the black water and brought to life the dark bayou. The old man lifted his face to the sky and let the rain wash the dirt from his wrinkled face. He ran his hands through his beard and scrubbed the grey clean with the rainwater. The drops of rain were large and cold. The coolness seeped into his worn body, welcome and refreshing.

When he looked to the water again, the orange bobber was gone, and the tip of the pole bent towards the water.

"We got him, Jess! Wooo!"

Quick as a young man, he grabbed the pole and raised it out of the water. The line was heavy and his back struggled to lift it. The orange bobber appeared first. He pulled harder, the catch heavy and hidden by the black water. He arched his back and pulled with all the strength left in his frail, thin arms. "He's a big one! Wooo!"

Finally, he lifted his hook out of the water and saw the turtle, large backed and heavy, appear on the end of the line. When the old man lifted the turtle out of the water, the turtle let go of the hook and dropped into the water, leaving the rusty hook swinging empty in the wind driven rain.

"He got us again, Jess," the old man said. He stared into the water, rain-soaked and tired. "Guess we'll have to try again tomorrow."

The wind calmed, but the rain fell harder. The old man turned and walked back up the trail into the woods. The trail was muddy now, and it made the walk back more difficult. About a mile up the trail, he came to a blue tarp strung between two trees. Under the tarp, there were cardboard boxes laid flat atop the mud, and various brands of beer cans strewn across the ground. He leaned the cane pole against a tree and crawled under the tarp. The old man took off his soaked shirt and wiped it across his weary forehead. He wiped his arms and his naked chest and bundled the shirt into a ball as he laid down on the cardboard. He put the balled-up shirt under his head and stared up at the tarp, listening to the rain crash against the fabric. Maybe the rain will bring more worms, he thought. His stomach rumbled.

"Tomorrow will be better, Jess," he said, staring at the tarp, alone and wet. The old man closed his tired eyes, felt his worn body, aching and cold, pressed hard against the cardboard. He thought of Jess and their life together, when they were happy and things were different. The thought warmed him.

The old man dropped to sleep. The rain crashed against the blue tarp and the thunder rumbled in the distance.

The Beach House

Written by Mary Jane Hill

I had not seen Dan in six years, not since the funeral in which he was the grieving husband, quiet and stoic as always. I wondered then how deep his loss felt to him, but I was too afraid to ask, too afraid to hear it was greater than I hoped, or that it was less than most believed.

My friends knew Dan as the older gentleman whose grandson befriended my son one summer while both attended camp together. No one realized that my friendship with Dan had gradually grown from the talk of everyday activities to more serious subjects. One afternoon when Dan unexpectedly invited me to lunch, he learned that I was feeling trapped in an unhappy marriage.

From that point on, Dan and I grew closer. As I fell in love with him, we both knew we couldn't be together. Dan let me set the pace of our relationship and when I feigned a decreasing interest in him, he did not ask questions. There was never a formal goodbye, only the memories of hopes that never materialized and dreams that were too difficult to face close up.

Dan and I never lost contact, though, so when his wife passed away suddenly, he let me know. We spoke very little then.

Time passed as it always does. Simple conversations with Dan separated long silences between us. I couldn't tell if he was lost or doing well. He didn't talk much of himself, but instead focused on me and how I was handling my life.

Dan's call came as a tremendous surprise to me a week ago. He was not willing to answer my questions directly, but this I understood about him. He and I had come to enjoy a language of nuances and subtle inferences early in our relationship when we fought to keep our growing closeness from turning into a secret intimacy.

Now, here I was driving to meet Dan on a damp winter night that would certainly chase away most beachgoers eager to smell the salty air or dig their feet in the cool sand. Surely Dan had a reason for choosing this coastal location. He never did anything without a reason.

Soon we were about to see each other again. I wondered what would happen and why he invited me here. I continued to ponder these thoughts as I approached our meeting place.

The house sat at the end of a narrow street with only sand separating it from the ocean. In the darkness I could see the porch light illuminating the exterior of the home, which appeared to be well-cared for. It had a cozy look I found appealing, but it wasn't quite Dan's style. Under the porch light sat a large pot of lavender flowers. I smiled at the sight of the petunias. Dan jokingly called all flowers petunias, and not only were these actually petunias, they were also my favorite color. I was beginning to feel there might be more to this meeting than I first wanted to let myself believe. That thought frightened me and my heart began beating a little faster.

As I parked in front of the house, the door opened and behind it stood Dan. His hair was gray now without any hints of the brown I remembered. His beard had turned all white and was shorter than he usually wore it, but it was the way he knew I most liked seeing him. My eyes stung as I recalled memories of a visit in which he wore his beard this way.

I was already smiling as I walked quickly toward him. He came outside, and as we approached each other I saw the affection in his eyes that was so often in contrast to his otherwise serious expression. In silence, we reached each other with arms outstretched and then his arms were around me holding me tightly, giving me that comfort I had been missing for so long.

I don't know how long we stood there, unable to let go, unable to speak, so many emotions flowing between us as they always had when we were together. The passage of time had not done anything to change that. This man had touched my life in a way no one else ever had and yet, in some ways, he was still such a stranger to me. What we shared was a mystery to both of us.

I didn't hear the crashing sounds of the nearby waves or the call of the seagulls on the deserted beach. I was only aware of the man whose arms held me, the familiar scent I identified only with him, the love overflowing from deep within my heart.

Then he whispered words I never heard him say before: "I've missed you." And before I could respond he said again, "I've missed you." It was then I knew why he had called me here tonight.

I held his arm as we walked toward the house, sometimes leaning my head against his shoulder. I commented on the petunias and he smiled for the first time. "You were always my 'Lavender Lady'." Hearing the affectionate name he'd given me years earlier reassured me some things never change.

Once inside, he guided me through a sparsely decorated, but very spacious, living room to a sliding glass door in the back. Opening it, he took my hand as we walked out onto a balcony with a beautiful ocean view. The full moon lit up the back of the house very well. I could see the waves approaching and crashing repeatedly.

We leaned against the railing at the far end of the balcony. He stood with his arm pressed against mine. I could only briefly glance at the waves before looking at Dan's profile. It was hard to believe so many years had gone by without seeing him.

I spoke first amidst a smile, "I'm looking at you, you know."

He raised one eyebrow, looking at me from the side and pretending he was only now aware of my stares. I giggled. Dan always had a way of making me laugh.

"You're analyzing," he said.

"Yes, that's me, always trying to figure things out."

He took a deep breath and turned to face me. Putting his hands on my arms and turning me toward him, he said, "I've had a lot of time to think. I always said I would wait for you unless you called to tell me you're not coming. Well, you've never made that call." My palms were sweating, my heart was pounding, and tears sat on the rim of my eyes.

I waited for him to say more, but he only gave me that familiar stare. "Dan, what is it you're trying to tell me? I'm not leaving here until you tell me why you asked me here."

He let go of my arms and turned back toward the ocean. I got scared this was suddenly going nowhere.

He continued staring at the ocean.

"Dan, please…."

"You like the ocean, don't you?"

"You know I do but what does that have to do with anything?"

He had such a difficult time expressing his feelings. Finally, he spoke.

"Remember when you first told me you had a dream… a dream to someday own a beach house and eat breakfast on a balcony that overlooked the ocean?"

"You remember that?"

He nodded. "I also remember telling you I couldn't buy a house for you without others noticing. Now no one is here to notice."

I wanted to believe I knew what he was saying, but I was too afraid to make any assumptions. "Dan, what are you telling me?"

"I bought this house, Allie… for you. It's yours if you want it. I've been sitting on that couch in there every night for the past month and not once did you call to tell me you weren't coming. And now you're here, but I don't have to stay. I can go."

I was speechless.

"I'm an old man now, Allie. I can never offer you what I could have if we had met earlier in our lives. You know that. But what I've never told you is that I've always loved you and that is why I tried so hard to do what was best for you. Buying this house is my way of trying to make up for all the things we've missed along the way. Will you accept it?"

My life would never be the same after that question. Dan and I held each other for hours, too afraid we might miss one more second of togetherness.

When it was time for me to leave, Dan encouraged me to give myself the happiness I had been longing for all the years he had known me. For the first time, I felt I might actually be able to do that. I certainly wanted to try.

The Orchid

Written by Eric Ryan

Alice's hands were young once, strong and soft. Now though, opening the lid of the bygone steamer trunk, they sear, and she feels the pain in the marrow of her bones. She struggles to remember what is inside, or even if this trunk is hers to unlock. She raises a hand to her nose when the musty scent reaches her. None of this is familiar.

Among the dusty contents of the trunk, a white silk handkerchief catches her eye. When she reaches in and lifts it from the belly of the trunk, a haze of memories is released that floats towards her on the updraft. They hover around her in the air, spinning circles, and a spark ignites her from within. A strange sense of familiarity washes over her like meeting a stranger for the second time. She waves away the dust dancing on the sun streaks coming through the window and says his name.

"Johnny."

A lifetime separates her now from the last time she spoke that name. The weight of it lingers on her tongue, leaving a bittersweet taste she both recognizes and doesn't. Delicately unfolding the square of silk, she reveals an orchid, lying paper flat and preserved. Its body lifeless and withered. The delicate petals threaten to fall to pieces with the faintest breath. The feelings rush in. Her ears fill with the brassy sound of a big band. She remembers. She sees Johnny and hears his voice. She smells the city and feels his lips on hers. She first saw this orchid corsage when he slipped it onto her wrist that night so long ago, before he shipped off to England and then to France, never to return.

Bringing the mummified flower close to her face she smiles. She thought the orchid was lost but here it has lived in this trunk for all these years; hidden away with all the things that reminded her of 1944. The gentle pink spots on its petals were faded, the greens wilted. The colors leached into the white of the silk and formed unfamiliar patterns, leaving flaxen tinged petals to hang on the stem. The flower's allure still captured her despite its age and its tired appearance.

Cradling the orchid now, gently, careful not to destroy any of what remained, she sees his suddenly familiar shape leaning against the closet door, hidden in shadow. Her eyes widen at the glowing ember of his Lucky Strike as he draws on the cigarette. He is charming and dashing in his uniform. A wedge cap tilted slightly on his head just like she remembers. She feels young again with wild mischief in her eyes.

Alice begins to drift away and feels the sweet sensations all over again. The way he kissed her underneath the blossoming magnolias in Central Park as the pink petals fell around them. How her white dress wafted out and spun as he twirled her, dancing and laughing. When the small bit of lace that held the orchid to her wrist had torn and she nearly lost the delicate flower in their elation. Kissing him again by the stone carved fountain as the water swelled and splashed back down in patterns, throwing millions of droplets into the air.

She met him earlier that day, but their time together was extraordinary, and he swept her off her feet. They were only given one night together before the troopship blasted its final call at dawn and she watched him swallowed by the steam on the Brooklyn docks with a green duffel over his shoulder.

With a final deep kiss and a tearful wave from the promenade deck, he was gone.

Under the orchid in the trunk was a sepia toned photo of a young man in his prime. His dark hair combed back and the radiant smile she could just now recall stretched ear to ear. She gave him a picture of her too, but she figured it was long gone now. Swallowed by hallowed waters and washed out to sea.

Alice lives another lifetime in these memories. She plants her feet in them and fights to stay. When she feels them pulling away, her pained fists clench the air, trying to grasp them before they leave her alone again in this empty room. Johnny's figure fades back into the shadow world and she reaches out towards it. With another blink he is gone, the light of his cigarette extinguished in the darkness. Her eyes close and she struggles to open them again. Both the sorrow and joy she feels are exhausting and the remaining energy she has deserts her.

Knowing she won't remember this she feels the fog returning. Before all is lost, she steals one last glance at the orchid and rests her head on the back of the rocking chair. "I remember." She whispers.

With the sound of those words she slowly closes her eyes and her hands fall gently to her sides, releasing the photograph and the orchid to sink slowly to the floor. She senses a hand intertwining with her own. She feels the touch of skin against her skin. Butterflies fill her belly as she begins to float. She can smell the metal and saltwater from Johnny's uniform in the air. Alice reaches down for the orchid as she rises but it has disappeared. She pays this no mind though because she can see that the road ahead is paved with them.

Disappearing Act

Written by Ryan Coull

Ian's hands trembled as he slumped into his Jaguar and eased down the electric window. He inhaled a few calming breaths of December night air. Drops of rain dampened his cheek. When he'd regained a little composure, he gunned the engine, which turned over smoothly, hit the lights, and edged from the drive, making a left. Squinting through his glasses, he accelerated up the street between denuded trees. His teeth ground together as his mind, unbidden, replayed Miriam's belligerent words.

Go on, get in your damn fancy car, do another disappearing act. Drive away like you always do. That's your answer to everything, isn't it? Go on, run away and practice your stupid magic tricks.

She called it running away; Ian called it his Time Out.

He was still shaking his head as he veered off Silverfern Road, where he and Miriam had stayed for better than eight years. On the surface, they lived an enviable life in the town's most affluent area—but their blessings went sailing over his wife's empty head. It mattered not that he'd purchased a beautiful four-bedroom house, an expensive car, five-star holidays and first-class flights, extortionate handbags and shoes that contented her only until the next design hit the shelves. All this and whatever else she dropped unsubtle hints for. Miriam took it all for granted, every single penny. Her limitless sense of entitlement kept dogged pace with the money he earned, as if she couldn't bear that there might be something in the pot to which she hadn't yet laid claim.

Ian drew up at a set of lights. The car in front had one of those "BABY ON BOARD" signs in the back. He shook his head. He couldn't understand the purpose of such things. How did one alter his driving to accommodate an infant in another car? It suggested people drove like maniacs unless aware of The Baby. It was almost insulting.

He looked left, where a pack of hooded youths idled outside a convenience store, the white splash from the electronic sign washing them in cold light. They swigged from bottles and called at each other, and Ian felt glad he wasn't that age any more.

The lights changed and he moved off.

Miriam wasn't the same person he'd married, bearing scant physical resemblance to the easygoing blonde he'd fallen for. He didn't expect her to be some sort of trophy wife, but she could at least make an effort. Where had it all gone awry? How had they ended up poles apart? At a mere thirty-two years old, he felt aged and distanced from the man he once was, so ground down that a weary resignation had seized hold of him.

He squinted under the blaze of oncoming headlights before activating the car's full beams, headed towards the town's outer limits. Rain thrummed on the roof. The car's interior was dark, dashboard dials and instruments illuminated in orange and red. He activated the CD player, and Dire Straits began "Your Latest Trick." But even music couldn't take his mind from her.

She was always having a go about something. Lately, not for the first time, it was his lifelong hobby—performing magic. He'd always enjoyed the process, the trickery, and although it was harmless enough, she wouldn't allow him even this simple indulgence.

When Ian was eight, his parents had presented him with a magic set for his birthday, complete with black top hat, wand, and cape. The gift had struck a chord, the interest took hold, and Ian spent hours every day rehearsing, posturing before the mirror, perfecting every flamboyant revelation until it became second nature. He had mastered those tricks—juvenile though they were—and gradually escalated his efforts to more challenging and visually impressive endeavours.

His teen sweetheart, Miriam, was the only thing Ian had worshipped more than performing tricks. When he lived with his parents, she would spray perfume on his pillow to make him think of her in her absence. Back then, before he'd landed his lucrative line-manager's position with a pharmaceutical company—Johnson and Johnson no less— they'd been at their happiest. Next they had rented a one bedroom apartment, earning little money with which to be frivolous, but they'd known contentment, and life had been great, for the most part. They'd had sex regularly, laughed a great deal, and it had seemed they always would. And Miriam had been supportive of his magic—or perhaps she'd only tolerated it. Yes, tolerated, as if expectant that he'd one day mature and realise magic had no place in a marriage. But should a person abandon a lifelong interest to please another?

Following the wedding and fortnight in Hawaii, Miriam had run to seed, as if he was no longer worth the effort. This had hurt, though Ian knew better than to broach such a thorny subject. Miriam's threshold for criticism was low, her response to it was disproportional and scathing. As time passed, she ballooned by four stone. She developed a habit of lounging around in anything with an elastic waist—when she wasn't parading her ever-increasing designer wardrobe in clubs and swanky restaurants. Her occasional cigarette became a pack a day—a habit he'd ditched in his twenties—and the lingering stench on her and the house was—

"Awful," he muttered, shaking his head. A lorry sped past in the opposite direction, buffeting the car. On the CD, the rising tempo of drums introduced "Money For Nothing."

She devoured chocolate, crisps, and Indian takeaway insatiably, and whiled away entire weeks watching soul-crushing soaps he couldn't abide. Failing that it was her blog and her Twitter account. Any common thread that existed between them had long since snapped. Their love life had suffered a slow death, as if every consumed chocolate robbed a little more libido—and the damned stuff was called an aphrodisiac. She ignored him much of the time, which he often chose to interpret as a kindness. When Miriam did bother with him, it was invariably to complain about him rehearsing tricks, or when she wanted something for the house.

What shade of drapes should we get in here, Ian? We need a Persian rug for over there, wouldn't you say? There's a grand Kashan I've had my eye on. It's hand knotted and a hundred percent wool. And we need some new scatter cushions, I saw satin ones with 3D-effect roses. For God's sake, Ian, you could at least show some interest. I know you'd rather be pulling satin hankies from your sleeve, but you can hear me, can't you?

And so it went, on and on. Listening to her, anybody would think she earned half the money; although she did nothing more than whittle it away on needless tat, most of which they had in abundance already. Their quarrels usually ended the same way: him getting in the car and driving around to cool off. His blessed Time Out. It annoyed the hell out of her, so Ian drew pleasure in doing it all the more. Far better than wading into another no-win debate. The truth was she no longer loved him, and vice-versa, a situation not uncommon on the rocky road called marriage. But Miriam had accustomed herself to having everything, and intimated that she'd fleece him for it all should they separate.

Some of the blame stopped with him, of course.

Marital problems are rarely one-sided. He'd given her everything she'd asked for, after all. It was easier to buy her the damned Kashan rug and scatter cushions and whatever materialistic clutter she craved. He'd tried denying Miriam before, but she'd caused such an almighty stink that it wasn't worth the trouble. Maybe she was testing him, though—Ian knew women did this sometimes, to ascertain whether their man would stand his ground. Well, he didn't have the patience for her button-pushing, not any more.

Palming a beat on the steering wheel, he followed the endless centreline and cats eyes that receded into the night, straining to see through his prescription lenses, his neck jutted out towards the windshield. Clustered spruce trees flitted past behind split-rail fences. The rain was thickening to sleet, teeming in the headlamps. It all made him feel depressed. The more he tried not to think of Miriam . . . the more he thought of her.

She picked away at him all the time. Pick-pick-pick. Only this morning she'd had another tiresome dig about his magic.

"Why don't you get a proper hobby?" she'd said, working her way through a tub of chocolate ice cream. "You could do something manly instead of—of shuffling cards and making stupid coins vanish."

"I like tricks," he told her. "What's wrong with tricks?"

"For God's sake, Ian, what're you like?"

"I liked magic when you married me, Miriam."

"You're such a wet blanket."

Pick-pick-pick.

Miriam didn't understand the buzz he got from well-executed tricks. Typically, she didn't appreciate the time and effort invested in getting the sleight of hand just right. Why would she? She couldn't even appreciate the time and effort it took to earn the money she drew so much pleasure in frittering away. In an attempt to please her—was that even possible?—he sometimes tried to involve her in the magic, but she complained and disliked the rigmarole of following instruction. She found the process awkward, time-consuming, and embarrassing besides—and although he persevered, she just wasn't interested. She'd forget which card she'd picked or ruin an illusion because she wouldn't concentrate, and Ian knew this was directly to needle him rather than any genuine failure on her part.

He dipped his beams as another lorry hurtled past, sluicing rainwater across the windscreen in its wake. The wipers lunged back and forth. He slipped his thumb and index finger beneath his glasses, rubbed at his eyes.

They no longer even socialized together. On rare evenings, Ian ventured out with friends. He had to ask Miriam along, of course, aware she always refused. She'd tell him to go and have a good time, and the next day he'd endure the silent treatment and the full force of petulance, as if he'd wantonly abandoned her to go out boozing.

Thankfully they'd never had children—kids would've only

complicated matters further. Miriam had never revealed a maternal side, and judging by the infrequency of their coupling, motherhood wasn't a priority. Perhaps she simply didn't want a family with him.

Ian's eyes went to the rear-view mirror, finding only darkness there. Coming down through the gears, he pulled off the main road, following a makeshift track into the trees, loose stones clanking against the manifold. The headlamps found a small, pale animal as it scampered across his path, and the startled incandescent eyes of another. The Jag jounced along the rutted way a little farther before Ian doused the lights and shut off the engine, silencing Dire Straits mid-song.

He listened to the faint sounds of the engine cooling before alighting from the car, raising his collar against the cold. The sleet had petered out. Glistening silver birches swayed in the chill breeze. Stream water whispered somewhere close by. The winter sky held a gibbous moon and was dappled with stars. He heard the faraway engines of a descending plane. He plucked off his glasses and went at them with a handkerchief from his jacket, his breath forming in little clouds. Amber orbs of distorted light identified the town, several miles in the distance.

Ian examined the lenses and slipped them back on. As he blinked, the town's far-off glows sharpened into focus. He stepped around to the boot, lifted it open, and stared inside at the heavyset form wrapped in the Kashan rug. A hundred percent wool it was. Hand knotted.

"You always hated magic," he said. "But you'll be part of my greatest ever trick, Miriam, dearest."

Ian withdrew the shovel, eased down the boot, and strode purposefully into the woods, about to perform the ultimate disappearing act.

About the Authors

Raissa Batra - Raissa Batra, born in 2006, hails from Patiala, in the north Indian state of Punjab. She sees herself as a budding wordsmith connecting to the world which has short stories and using her craft to speak up against discrimination of all kinds — gender, racial, or economic. She also loves to play the piano and firmly believes that writing is a lot like music — to make an impact one must strike the right notes.

Ryan Coull - Ryan Coull has published stories in The New Writer, Firstwriter, and Scribble magazine, as well as in anthologies such as 'An Eclectic Mix Volume Four' and 'On the Day of the Dead'. His story 'Garage 54' won the Swansea and District Writers' Circle short story competition in 2015 and was released in an e-book of the same name. He has a collection of tales under the title 'A Grave Temptation and Other Stories'.

Milo Cumaranatunge - Milo is an engineer by training and currently works in R&D at a technology company in Minnesota. He is a storyteller at heart and has always been interested in the written word. When he escapes the Midwest winters to bake under the Sri Lankan sun, his country of birth, he has occasionally written and published journalistic articles in a national newspaper there. Milo serves on the board of directors at Graywolf Press in Minneapolis and is an advocate for small independent publishing houses.

Clay Harris - I am a high school social studies teacher in Baton Rouge, LA. I live in Ascension Parish with my beautiful wife and two constantly hungry children. I've always wanted to write, but life kept getting in the way. Until one day, I decided to push life aside, pick up my pencil, and start.

Barbara M Herrera - Barbara Herrera is a writer first, a human second, and a horror lover third. As a simultaneous English major, digital copywriter, blogger, and fiction author, most of her time is spent immersed in the written word. When she's not reading or writing, she can often be found watching the birds in her California backyard or overanalyzing a movie with her always-supportive wife, Brianna.

Mary Jane Hill - After growing up in New Jersey, Mary Jane attended college in southern California, which is now her permanent home. She shares a century-old house with her husband, two adult children, and a happy dog who loves car rides. Mary Jane enjoys the flexibility of being an independent bookkeeper which allows her time to focus on writing short stories and poetry. She is also working on a historical fiction novel.

Debra S. Jacobs - Born in Kew Gardens, New York, Debra has lived for the past many decades in the Sonoran Desert. She has enjoyed a varied career as an occupational therapist and now, as her OT career will be coming to an end in the next few years, she hopes to add to her author credits a mystery series and historical fiction. Debra has published two non-fiction titles in her field of working with children with special needs. Debra is inspired by the peace and natural beauty around her. She lives with her husband and sweet dog Buddy.

Claire A Murray - Claire writes short and long stories in several genres. "Lucky Seven" and "The Backpack" (So West: Lady Killers, Fall 20201) are her 8th and 9th published short stories. "Spirit in the Sky" (Peace, Love, and Crime: Crime Fiction Inspired by the Songs of the '60s), released in November 2020. Claire is a member of Sisters in Crime and its Guppy, New England, Desert Sleuths, and LA chapters, and the Short Mystery Fiction Society. A lifelong New Englander, she moved in mid-2020 to Arizona where she writes full time. Website: https://cam-writes.com, Where Character, Crime, and Mystery Collide.

Carrington Parrott - Carrington Parrott is a young adult who has always had a passion for reading and writing. She was born in Canada and raised in the United States, mostly in Texas. As a college student, she started attending university in Arizona state and now currently resides in New York where she serves in the US Army and is continuing her degree. She is proud to be having her first short story published and beyond humbled to share it with fellow readers.

L. Player - L. Player is an author of flash and short fiction. She was born in Brooklyn and began writing at 14 and has gone on to publish books and stories. Inspired by S.E. Hinton she published a book of poetry at age 16. Most recently she has placed in the University of San Francisco's writing competition and has published a journal entitled, 'My COVID-19 Journal'.

You can find more information on her website at the following link: linktr.ee/lplayer

P.A. Richardson - Originally from the Midwest, Patricia Richardson is a fiction writer and poet now living in northwest Washington. She takes advantage of the gorgeous backdrop of the Salish sea and the Cascade mountain range to tell tales ranging from vignettes of everyday life to metaphysical mysteries. In her spare time, Patricia enjoys learning tarot, playing poker, hanging out with friends and family, and exploring the beauty of the Pacific Northwest.

Eric Ryan - Eric Ryan and his family live just north of Boston on the New England coast in the shadows of Salem Village, the Rebecca Nurse Homestead, and Lovecraft's Arkham Asylum. After studying screenwriting and film production at the School of Visual Arts, he served three years in the US Army and is a veteran of the war in Iraq. By day he works as a Boston Firefighter and by night he chases his children around before settling down to write short stories and finish his first novel.

Ramona Scarborough - Ramona Scarborough has published eleven novels in different genres: romance, suspense, historical, amusing nostalgia, and a collection of short stories. Her stories and articles have appeared in over one-hundred magazines, anthologies, and online venues. Her work mainly focuses on love, relationships, and family. She lives in Salem, Oregon with her husband, Chris, and their two rescue cats.

Adam Silver - I've always have loved telling stories, having started at an early age when I entertained fellow vacationers in the Catskills stories that popped up in my imagination. As a student, I was always known for my writing ability, a love that continues to this day. Writing is something that never left me, and I look forward to exploring where it will take me.

Joshua Zepnick - An avid lover of poetry and 19th-century literature, Josh Zepnick is working on finishing his Bachelor's degree in English through Arizona State online. He resides in Green Bay, Wisconsin, and works at Cintas. In his free time, he enjoys reading, writing, and long walks just about anywhere except the beach.

MORE FROM CITY LIMITS PUBLISHING

Six years of writings sat unfinished until COVID-19 gave Robert Martin the time needed to finish the job. *In Idled Stacks: A Collection of Poetry* provides a glimpse into the life and mind of the author. Featuring poetry about the Coronavirus pandemic, racial civil unrest, relationships, life's storms, and more, In Idled Stacks is an emotional and fascinating look into the life of the everyman.

Dances with Words, a collection of over 500 haiku speaks to the pathos, pain, and passion of this journey we call life. Random thoughts, rants, raves, reminiscences, prayers of praise, et al – framed in poetic bite-size bits – 17 syllables at a time. Built around song titles and lyrics, the writer weaves themes that touch the deepest part of us. Love, God's love, forgiveness, tears, sadness, healing and loss – et al. My prayer is that my passion and pathos – my loves and losses can speak to you, wherever you are – whatever your story.

Leave the present behind and journey with us to another place, another time. This collection of short stories featuring fantasy and fairytales represents over a dozen authors and stories. Meet the Woman with No Name in Lady Summerfeld: A Fable. Find your purpose with Franz in A Magnificent Sanctuary. Go on The Hunt with Jagr. Come of age in Fairie with Faye. The possibilities are endless, the paths are winding, and the journeys are thrilling. Explore *Another Place, Another Time* today.

Poems of Political Protest: An Anthology is a collection of poems by various authors who are attempting to make their own waves in their community and in the global community. They're the words of the hurting, the fighting, and the driving force behind real and impactful change. All we have, all we own freely and clearly, are our words. May this collection bring about action.

An emotionally scarred woman in 2019 gets the chance to go back in time to stop a terrible tragedy. But there's a catch: she must overcome her insecurities and learn to trust people — and herself — in order to save dozens of innocent lives. Brenda Lyne lives just outside Minneapolis, Minnesota with her two kids and two cats. *Charlie's Mirror* is her first novel, and she believes it is never too late to follow your dreams.

CPSIA information can be obtained
at www.ICGtesting.com
Printed in the USA
FSHW011026310121
78144FS